The Rogue Cell

A Novel

M.E. Shaw

The Rogue Cell is a work of fiction. Names, characters, places, and incidents are the products of the author's imagination or are used fictitiously. Any resemblance to actual events, locales, or persons, living or dead, is entirely coincidental.

Copyright © 2014 by M.E. Shaw.

All rights reserved.

No part of this book may be reproduced, scanned, or distributed in any printed or electronic form without permission of the author. Please do not participate in or encourage piracy of copyrighted materials in violation of the author's rights. Purchase only authorized editions.

ISBN-13: 978-1495282263
ISBN-10: 1495282260

ACKNOWLEDGMENTS

I want to thank my very supportive husband, Rosendo for his unwavering encouragement over the last three years as I struggled to complete this novel. He never doubted that I would publish this book, but as time flew by, he began to gently push me.

I also want to thank a generous childhood friend, Cheryl Albig who just happened to be a talented line editor who took on my manuscript and assisted this novice. Another thank you goes to my beta reader, Ashley Shimp, for her invaluable critique.

And lastly, I want to thank my beloved daughter, Paula Bagwell Knipp, who formatted my manuscript, created the book cover and did the final touches for publishing.

Allowing my day job and life adventures to sidetrack me for months at a time, I eventually focused my efforts to let my characters come alive and tell their story.

M.E. Shaw

In memory of my mom, Evelyn Shaw, my greatest supporter

PROLOGUE

The delivery van, identified only by a small medical caduceus emblem on the driver's door, stopped before the enormous, black gate at the entrance to the compound.

"Here's some more for ya," called out the driver to the guard as he jumped out of the van and slid open the side panel. He picked up three small bags from a refrigerated container.

"We've been slammed lately," said the guard as he reached for the bags. "And you're getting to be a regular," he added.

"I know," the driver said, laughing. "I don't know what was going on nine months ago. Did we have a power outage or something?" He quickly scanned each bag with his electronic pad, slammed the panel shut, and got back into the van. "You probably have not seen the last of me this week," he said as he waved a good-bye and drove off.

The onslaught was even more evident as the guard walked into the building with his precious cargo. Technicians scurried around to accommodate the influx of new arrivals.

"Sid, how many you got for us this time?" asked Tad as he greeted the guard at the intake counter. Tad, dressed in a space-age jumpsuit, shook his hand and patted him on the shoulder. He took the specimens of placentas, umbilical cords and cord blood, handing them to a clerk for admission.

"Three. Carl said it's not over, Tad, more to come. He's on call for five additional hospitals. When it rains, it pours," he said laughing.

"Bring 'em on," said Tad, with an impish smile. "We can handle as many as they can send us." He had been an expert in the field of birthing clones since its inception thirty years ago. And it never got old.

He was one of only a handful of humans to be involved in the inner workings of the process. Fifty percent of the workforce was now comprised of clones. He worked and lived with them, rarely needing to venture outside the walls.

The building appeared massive from the outside, encapsulated with super-strength materials sturdy enough to withstand any event Mother Nature could throw its way, including tornadoes, category-five hurricanes and even earthquakes. Masking its strength, it wore a refined, elegant veneer of stone and marble, resembling a fine Italian mansion. Gardens surrounding the factory were in constant bloom with vibrant colors from spring through fall. Walkways winded endlessly throughout, flanked by gentle streams meandering under the majestic old oaks and maple trees. The lush grass gave a fresh scent. One hundred feet past the facility was another wall. Built with large sandstones, it rose to sixteen feet. A golden plaque engraved with "Community 27" adorned a thick, solid gate. Armed guards surrounded the entrance.

Belying its exterior, the extensive inside incorporated a processing plant of sorts.

"Ready, Tad," said the intake clerk as he handed the bags back over to Tad.

Scooping them up, Tad called on his wrist intercom. "Jack, I'm bringing three to your station." No time was wasted in starting the processing.

The Reproductive Department, the size of a warehouse, was comprised of dozens of stations manned by expert technicians and overseen by researchers responsible for twenty stations each. At the stations, stem cells were extracted from the newly arrived human material to begin the process of regeneration, a marvelous journey to develop a perfect, identical clone of a newborn human. Along with the birth byproducts was a microchip the size of a grain of rice, an exact copy of the one already placed in a corresponding newborn.

After depositing the bags with Jack, Tad walked briskly to the adjacent Growth Lab. Hundreds of three-foot by three-foot glass cylinders filled, with life-sustaining fluid, and lined up in multiple rows, revealed neophyte clones in varying stages of development. The immense room neared capacity of developing fetuses.

Tad peered into one unit with a hefty-looking fetus floating in the synthetic, amniotic fluid, filling the artificial womb almost to its limit. "You're a big bruiser," he snickered. It never ceased to amaze him how it took just two weeks to go from one cell to a full-term, fully breathing, crying baby; a clone baby.

An alarm chimed. One of the clone babies had reached full-term. A technician immediately rushed over, checked the monitoring equipment and prepared for the delivery.

An experienced delivery nurse joined the technician, checking all the fetal parameters before the final step in the birthing process. "Hello there, little one. Looks like you're ready to join the world."

"All set," said the technician as he emptied the tank. The nurse plucked the baby out and stimulated it until it cried hardily. "You're a big noise maker," she said, laughing, "but perfect, I hope."

The curly brown-haired baby hit the scale at seven pounds, five ounces and looked adorable with a tiny turned-up nose. She soon settled down as she was bundled in a warm, soft blanket. The nurse took the baby to an adjacent room, the Evaluation Station, and examined her carefully, using an APGAR test to record all her functions and status. Although developed in the 1950s for human newborns by Dr. Apgar, its parameters remained pertinent for evaluation of both humans and clones: Appearance, Pulse, Grimace, Activity, and Respiration. Additional criteria had been added for the clone babies. A baby's demeanor was tested as well as its capacity to be comforted. A clone baby had the rare ability to self-comfort, and fussiness rarely occurred.

"She's a beauty," Tad commented to the nurse as he peered over her shoulder. "I hope she aces all her tests. You look like a sure thing," he said to the now cooing baby girl. "Got to get back to Intake, expecting more deliveries."

One procedure remained; brain alteration. This tweaking augmented the genetic predestination and assured that the clone possessed the psychological adjustment from birth to live a life of contentment with its sole purpose of providing replacement parts for its original human, or OH, as they commonly were called. Although clones were inherently happy and compliant, this quick step insured that the brain had no chance of becoming otherwise. The tiny microchip would be implanted in the arm at this time.

The operating room had a dozen individual cubicles for

conducting the surgical procedures. The nurse whisked the newly birthed clone to cubicle six for the final steps.

The surgeon moved from cubicle five to cubicle six, changing sterile gloves as he walked, and within seconds, the temporal lobe was entered, lasered and subsequently closed, and a steri-strip was placed over the tiny incision. He then quickly inserted the microchip and pronounced, "Everything is snipped, placed and patched," as he pulled off his gloves and proceeded to cubicle seven.

The nurse cuddled the newborn and took her to the Clone Nursery. Within an hour, the baby happily devoured fortified soymilk. Cradling and rocking her in her arms, she said, "You darling thing. You soon will be going to your loving clone parents. They are anxiously waiting for you."

This scenario occurred without a hitch nine times out of ten, provided the baby passed the final quality control assessment. If, for some reason, the baby failed this last step, it would be disposed of, and the regeneration process would be started all over again.

CHAPTER 1

Abby picked up the ornate envelope; the seal of the New World Order emblazoned on it in the upper left corner, the address written in fancy script, Ms. Abigail 84528. The impact of the request still shook her to her core. On the other hand, she rationalized, it gave her the opportunity to really shine. But no time today to deal with it, she groaned to herself. I have my priorities and today we are welcoming a baby. She threw it back down on the counter.

"I guess we're all ready for our little cherub," Abby announced to herself as no one else was even in earshot. She stopped at the kitchen sink, grabbed a soapy cloth, running it over the counters for the third time, then toweled them dry, examining each to be sure there were no smudges. Her natural white-blond hair was pulled up into a ponytail, tendrils falling out around her hairline.

"Peyton," yelled Abby, trying to find her housemate. "I can't wait to see this baby." Abby stopped to rock the little bassinette. It was set up in the kitchen, as that was where everyone usually congregated.

Peyton came bounding around the corner into the kitchen. "Abby, would you calm down? One would think you were going to be the new mother to this little one." She grabbed Abby by the shoulders, turned her around and marched her to a counter chair. "Now sit for two seconds," she demanded.

"I can't help it," Abby said. "You know how I am," she protested, raising her shoulders in a shrug.

Exasperated, Peyton scowled at her in feigned displeasure.

Peyton and Abby, although not from the same DNA, were as good as sisters. But they were as different as day and night. Ironically, they were birthed on the same day, twenty-eight years ago, arrived at the same time, and were brought up in the same house and family. Not only were they quasi sisters, they were best friends. And they were clones. The two of them were a perfect team, each complementing the other; Peyton calming Abby down, and Abby nagging Peyton. They laughed a lot and learned from each other.

Peyton wore her long, gently curling, sable hair down today, hanging just below her shoulders. She shot Abby a look with wide, expressive eyes, a deep brown shade resembling coffee beans and outlined by black, long lashes Her skin, a Mediterranean golden-tan, complemented a slim, but curvy body. Her height was 5' 6", not overly tall, but statuesque nonetheless. She towered over Abby but then, most people did. Her DNA provided Italian features, which she favored most, and French, maybe accounting for her love of and fluency in French. She had a gentle nature about her, soft-spoken, elegant, and articulate, with a vocabulary indicative of a good education.

"Are Claire and Barron as giddy as you?" asked Peyton. She had not seen them all day. "They haven't had a baby in the house for a few years now. I hope they're up to the sleepless nights." She slid into a chair at the counter and watched Abby, now busy at work, preparing dinner for a change.

"You know those two," answered Abby, quickly cutting vegetables at the sink. "They're taking it in stride like everything else around here. But yes, they are really getting excited. So are the twins. They won't be the babies anymore. About time too, since they're six years old," she said laughing.

"It's so nice of you to do the dinner tonight for Claire. I'm sure Claire and Barron are still finishing last-minute preparations." Peyton threw Abby a warm smile.

Abby used her arm to wipe her hair out of her heart-shaped face, highlighted by a peaches and cream complexion. She went to the pantry and attempted to reach a jar of homegrown, canned tomatoes and failed. Peyton walked over and easily retrieved it. "You shrimp," she said as she handed it to her.

Even though their beauty and figures in human terms would have put them in a class of supermodels, their looks here at the community were not very important. There was, however, certainly competition for life partners. Both Abby and Peyton were pursued constantly, but with their all-consuming schedules, neither one of them felt compelled to link up yet.

Abby and Peyton shared the spacious five thousand square-foot home with four other adults, two of whom had raised them, and six children of varying ages. Now they were expecting one more to add to the mix.

Peyton continued to watch Abby slave away, with no offer to help. She thought about the prospect of having a new baby in the house. So far, Abby and Peyton had always had the dubious honor of being aunts to the little ones, which suited them just fine. Personally, they'd rather have their four legged precious cats and dog to care for than little two-legged clone babies.

As if on cue, Beavis, their little Pomeranian trotted in. He danced on his two hind feet, begging for a treat. He was a puff of white fur about the size of a medium-sized cat. In fact, he was smaller than their two cats that were now lazily lying on the wide windowsill of the breakfast room. They all got along wonderfully in spite of the advantage the cats had over this diminutive creature.

Peyton slid off her chair to fetch a snack for Beavis. "You're constantly eating, Beavie, yet you are such a tiny thing. At least you don't wake us up at night to eat every two hours." She returned to her chair and rested her chin on her hands with both elbows on the counter. She had been working from home for a few hours and was pretty much drained.

"You look beat, Peyton. And, don't worry, you don't need to help me. I've got it all under control." She knew she wasn't going to get an offer anyway as she gave her a sideways glance with an exaggerated pained look.

"Thanks, Abs. What I really should do is go out for a run." She was already dressed in sweats, but then thought better of it. "Nah, on second thought, I think I'll just stay here and watch you work." Abby leaned over and gave her a punch.

Peyton yawned, stretched and continued to stare at Abby. She then reached over and picked up the envelope. She re-read the announcement. Her mind drifted off momentarily. She felt so safe in their community. There was absolutely no contact or communication with humans other than designated, highly classified, human officers. No one had ever been permitted on the grounds. Besides the few highly classified humans working in the creation laboratory just outside the main entrance, all contact had been from the community designee going outside the borders to meet. Now, under highly unusual circumstances, that rule was about to change…like the change coming up in a couple of weeks, according to the announcement. So, in addition to getting the house ready for a newborn, Peyton and Abby were in the midst of preparing the community for very special guests. Human guests.

CHAPTER 2

The day started crisp and cool. The rolling hills and fresh air were the respite he needed just about now. He kicked off his shoes, stretched and took in a deep breath. "Ahhh, it's such a relief to have these few hours of solitude," he said to his driver, Andre. Andre took a brief look in his rear view mirror to see Johann finally relaxing after months of non-stop work. "Don't get me wrong, Andre, I do love my work, but once in a while a guy needs a break." Andre smiled, nodding in agreement.

They were on their way to a community in south central New York. The best part was that he was meeting up with his good friend, Miguel Tavares, who just happened to be the President of the New World Order, the governing body of the entire world. How lucky that he, Dr. Johann Christiansen, ended up in this position so early in his career.

Being too keyed up to sleep, his thoughts started to drift to an earlier time, eight years ago, when he was at Harvard Medical School. He remembered a particular class in biogenetics where his professor expounded on the marvelous scientific advances of the day and on how civilization had been transformed.

"In 2009, President Barack Obama managed to overturn the ban on stem cell research. That major event gave way to a frenzy of research in the U.S. Other countries had already cloned humans, but the results had been abominable. Tons of genetic errors occurred with inevitable deaths and deformities resulting. It was a disaster. With the U.S. coming into the equation, things turned around dramatically."

Another professor added, "I was a young doctoral student in 2004 when the FDA approved the implantable, rice grain-sized microchip for use in humans. That also was a big deal back then. It seems so primitive compared to what we use today. The tiny subcutaneous RFID chip was being made by HumiChip, which is still in operation, but now with lots of competition." He laughed, "They were marketing it as a life-saving device back then. What a hard sell that was. Many people thought it was creepy."

A student spoke up, "How could they not see the advantages, like what a fantastic future it held? It has proven to be such an asset for retrieving medical info when a patient comes into the ER unconscious or for discouraging would-be kidnappers or finding people who are lost or missing."

Another student piped up, "I can't imagine a time when humans did not have a chip in their bodies. I guess back then there wasn't much trust in the government, and people feared that they would be spied on from a hostile government agency."

The first student agreed adding, "Well, the government does, in fact, spy on us, but it is done with good intentions and only when absolutely necessary. I guess we are accustomed to it and don't feel our liberties are being taken away. Besides, look at the good it has done. It sure has eliminated terrorists from our world."

"Yeah, they could run, but they couldn't hide. That sure was a scary time in our history. I'm glad I was born after all that bloodshed and transformation."

The professor spoke up saying, "I remember when Mexico was the first to use RFIDs for eighteen members of the Attorney General's staff in order to control access to a new government facility. They also marketed it there to the people to stem the wave of abductions by drug cartels. They experienced at least three thousand kidnappings a year at the time. People were flocking to have a chip implanted in them."

"I read about that," replied another student. Laughing, he said, "My understanding is that at that time the scanners had to be within thirty feet to register. They would have needed scanners on every corner, in every building, to find anyone."

The first student said, "Well at least they could identify dead bodies!" The whole class roared.

The professor continued. "After a few years, the technology improved, and they were able to add global positioning to the chip and newer and better satellites that could track without failure. Even so, the earlier model worked well in prisons to keep track of inmates. Even some manufacturers used the system to keep track of employees in large warehouses, etc. Kept them on their toes, for sure."

"They must have had quite a time, what with the ethical questions and religious concerns that they had to muddle through," the second student added. "So glad we are past that and can continue to perfect the science."

"There was a huge setback, April 5, 2010," the professor explained, "when Senate Bill 235, prohibiting forced micro chipping in humans, was passed. It took quite a few years to change the mindset of the nation."

Johann had been engrossed listening to the discussion. Then the conversation changed.

The professor had now returned to the subject of the success of the cloning process. Johann had been entranced and knew then that he had found his future in medicine. He had already planned to specialize in internal medicine with a subspecialty in cloning or more technically, genetic proliferation. Now it was crystal clear he had picked the right specialty for his life career.

The car hit a small bump in the road, reorienting him to his whereabouts. They were getting closer to their destination. The hills were getting a little steeper, the vast valleys still visible down below. The lush fields were all around now. Birds flew overhead, heading to their nest and just enjoying the sunny day with their pals. *I envy the folks that witness this every day of their lives,* he thought to himself. The city life really wasn't his thing.

New to his position, he was thrilled to be visiting Community 27 as one of his first tasks. In fact, he was one of only a handful of officials of human society to be allowed inside the walls. And prior to today, admittance had been only to the creation factory, but not for him. He didn't even have clearance. No one had been allowed to observe the actual clone living conditions. In fact, the only information human society had been given was that the clones were created, but as far as most knew, they were kept in gigantic test tubes. It all was a mystery. He was one of only a few privileged persons to understand that they lived outside of their embryonic environment.

This community, he had learned, was exceptional and headed by a woman.

It was late morning now. They had gotten a pretty decent start. It was hard to get the few chosen dignitaries on the same page, out the door and into the various vehicles. But his assistant, Kirt Larson, was an exceptional organizer, managing to get everyone located, tagged and on their way. What would I do without him, he thought to himself. He not only keeps me on schedule, but he is also my best friend.

Kirt was a handsome, roguish dude, 6'2" with a shock of out of control blond hair and a thick German accent. He had been around Americans since a teenager, so was thoroughly fluent in English. He had a very colorful background–as famous seafarer and pilot. He flew all over the world as a private pilot for the rich and famous. His younger days were spent on the open seas off the coast of Europe teaching sailing on majestic vessels. Having been a top sailing captain, competing in races all over the world, his den displayed dozens of cups he had won.

Johann had known Kirt his whole life, meeting him through his relatives in Sweden as a young boy. Johann had spent all of his summers in Lulea, Sweden, and was totally fluent. He knew a smattering of German too, picked up from hanging out with Kirt

Now Kirt had a more regimented job, keeping Johann on schedule and on task. It was no easy thing, as Johann hated time constraints. In fact, he would not even wear a watch. If he absolutely needed to know the time, he would check his cell phone.

The partnership worked like hand in glove. Kirt was well compensated for his expertise too. He was only thirty-one but a millionaire already. This fact also kept the roadies lining up for an almost impossible, in fact, a fat chance, of having a date with him. Kirt was not into dating anyone right now as his job kept him too busy. He would occasionally have an attractive girl on his arm to attend public functions, but that was about it. He would love 'em and leave 'em, same as Johann.

The two of them had a great life, recently traveling the world over, visiting research labs, creation facilities, and meeting with heads of state. There would be plenty of time later to settle down with a family. That was a frequently repeated mantra Johann recited to his mom. Right now it really did not appeal to either of them.

And now they would be visiting and assessing clone communities worldwide. Could life get any more exciting? It was a dream come true. Johann sighed as he thought of the opportunity given him.

As they drove through the main gates of the community, Johann was amazed at what he saw: A sprawling maze of brilliant flowers, lush green lawns and in the background, vast pastures with beautiful horses and their foals. He could see other pastures in the distance with herds of cattle, which he thought strange as he recently learned that clones were vegetarians; in fact vegans, so would not even be using milk for consumption. That was one question he could not wait to ask.

They pulled up to the entrance of the library-education building. As he emerged from the car, he glanced around, feeling an incredible warmth surge through his body as he took in the enormous, earthen-stone entryway of soft gray and wheat hues. He wondered what architect genius designed this building. The ambience engulfed him, with its surrounding gardens, benches and multiple nooks for quiet reflection and meditation. He felt an instant calmness.

Hmmm, he thought to himself. I think this is going to be more intriguing than I had anticipated. He hid a deep grin behind his hand as he turned away to face the door.

What Johann did not know was that today was going to change the rest of his life, in fact, turn it upside down.

CHAPTER 3

Peyton arrived early knowing that today was the most important day in Community 27's history, besides its inception, that is.

It is not every day you have hordes of humans coming in to assess every aspect of our community, she sighed. She was ready, though, thanks to many weeks of preparation. Ever since receiving that letter, she and Abby had worked feverishly to make sure the community would showcase its attributes. Buildings were touched up with fresh, new paint. Gardens, even though painstakingly manicured at all times, were given extra care with additions of even more brilliant flowers. Uniforms and wardrobes were impeccably chosen to impress the dignitaries.

Now she was in her office and it wasn't even 7:00 am. The green smoothie she sipped would have to do for many hours, not that she was hungry. She rubbed her tummy, hoping to calm her nervousness The gigantic library that housed the core of the entire education system teamed with workers, arriving early to assure that the facility was in tip top shape for today's guests.

The expandable boardroom, now opened to the size of a ballroom, had crystal water glasses set up at each seat. Soon a buffet of vegetarian snacks, rice crackers, assorted fruits and vegetables and plentiful dips of all flavors and textures would be set out on beautiful platters of green and gold. It would also include finger sandwiches of chicken salad, which she understood was a favorite of this human species. Of course their guests would never be the wiser that the chicken really wasn't chicken. They had perfected the taste so that no one would be able to distinguish the switch. The meals were outstanding and rivaled any meat-based meal prepared by humans.

Peyton glanced at her watch, her mind now racing. Their expected ETA was 11:30 am. Abby would provide her opening remarks first, a compulsory synopsis of the operational function of our community. I will then be introduced and give my 'schpiel' and then be stuck with them for the rest of the day, she mused. She furled her brow, already anxious for the day to be over. In a sense she was excited about the history- making day, but also concerned it might change their lives; their comfortable, contented lives. Her face tightened as her concern escalated. She fidgeted with her necklace.

Oh Abby, she continued thinking, you have to help me with these humans— not that she feared being with the upper echelon of human specimens. She just had better things to do. She also had mixed feelings about them peering into their private world. She better get her thoughts together, in a positive vein, she scolded herself, as this was an opportune time to ask for things that her community needed.

They were totally self-sufficient for the most part, but occasionally they had to ask for things from the human world—like machinery or parts to fix machinery or updated high-tech items. Keeping current with technology was really a necessity for the library building and education system as a whole.

I'm sure humans think it silly for clones to have the best education possible, she thought. After all, our sole purpose is to lengthen their lives. You don't have to be particularly smart to do that. I bet that is what they assume as they have no idea what goes on behind our walls. Boy, are they in for a surprise. She had no idea that human society actually had no clue to their human-like existence.

Peyton let out a huge sigh. Why do I keep having these negative thoughts about humans and our role? She never heard anyone else uttering disparaging comments. She gathered her notes, trying to focus. She, as usual, put those uncharacteristic thoughts to the back of her mind, now concentrating on her upcoming speech.

She spotted Abby passing her door. "Hey girl," she shouted. "You better not leave me alone with this pack of wolves today."

"Peyton, my very accomplished and super capable friend," she shouted back, "you will be just fine. Besides, maybe one will be cute and you can convince your clone self to be attracted to him." She let out a huge burst of laughter, cupping her hand over her mouth.

"Okay, Abby, you nutcase. You're right," she admitted. "I can handle them," she shouted back. "And don't worry about my being attracted to a human. Ain'tgonna happen."

She straightened up her desk and looked around her attractive office with dark wood desk, credenza and bookcases. A laptop computer sat neatly on the corner of her desk. She used it mainly for visual monitoring of all the library and education facilities and Skyping as needed. Sure saved her a lot of time not having to physically traipse to each location or try to locate someone by phone. She could simply put in the person's individual ID code from their implanted chip and bingo, they were instantly displayed on her computer or arm pad. She would know their location and who they were with at any given moment. Peyton was very respectful of people's privacy, though, and only used this function for work matters.

Time was flitting away, now 10:30 am. She shuffled some papers on her desk. Where has the morning gone? she whined to herself. She had spent the morning going over her opening remarks and the tour schedule. Clones were posted at certain positions to answer questions all along the route. Of course, Abby prepared them in advance to be able to answer the inevitable questions that most likely would come up:

Are you happy here?

Is there anything you think can be improved?

Are you satisfied with the leadership? and on and on.

Putting plants in the crowd, again, was Abby's brilliant idea. Absently, she thought, that's why we are a good team. Abby instinctively thinks of clever details like that, that somehow elude my brain. She is a much more detailed-oriented person than I, darn it. Oh well, I am the people person, always trying to help the population if I can. Almost time, she thought as she again glanced at her watch.

Peyton walked out of her office to inspect the foyer where she would be greeting her guests. Fresh flower arrangements adorned the gargantuous earth tone pots. The brilliant colors of lavender, orange and yellows exuded an essence of the very impressive interior. The ceilings were sixteen feet high with windows all the way to the top, letting in streams of sunshine and illuminating framed pictures on the walls. The room was aglow with the warmth of that sunshine. Peyton had spared no expense when planning the decor of this massive building. It had to reflect a world of discovery and research that an education provided and the thirst for learning that even clones experienced.

One of the paintings displayed a portrait of the "father of cloning," Dr. James Bradley. No entrance would be complete without it, at least in this community. The rest of the collection was from famed clones who had inherited talent from their genes.

We will never know of the corresponding OH talent, Peyton thought pensively, as she peered at all the beautiful paintings that adorned the walls. It is not our prerogative to know our OHs' talents or how they live—we are only to serve them when the need arises, she recited silently to herself. "Everything seems in order here, so now all we need to do is wait," said Peyton, talking to no one in particular. She now hid her nervousness well.

Abby came clattering back in over the highly polished marble floors. "Abby, my dearest," said Peyton, "you could not have worn some quieter shoes?"

"Nah," Abby retorted, "these are sexier," as she winked at Peyton.

Peyton let out her familiar sigh. "You are a trip, Missy!"

An onslaught of black SUVs, town cars and limousines rolled up to the entrance, coming to a stop under the wide portico.

"Oh joy," commented Peyton. "Showtime!"

As they unloaded, the collection of dignitaries and bodyguards seemed to grow exponentially.

Peyton peered out frowning and said, "If any more cars pull up, we'll need Bob out there for crowd control."

Abby giggled, looking back at Peyton with a wide grin. Her eyes twinkled with excitement. "Yeah, it's quite a mob."

Suddenly, one particular guy stood out among the group. Not overly tall, maybe 5'11", but something about him caused Peyton to fix her beautiful, inquisitive eyes on him. "Hey, Abs, who is that intriguing one?"

"Ahaa, let me look in my cheat-book—I have pictures. That's Dr. Johann Christiansen, Director of the International Clone Federation. He's the head honcho, my dearest."

"So young? Are you sure?" Peyton questioned. She stared at

him, glad he couldn't see her gawking.

"Yup, got it right here," Abby said, flipping through her prep book.

Isn't it just like Abby, sighed Peyton, to assemble a bio book and be totally prepared to address these creatures like she has known them personally for years. "You are just too anal, Abs," Peyton quipped, "but man, I am so glad you are. You are my lifesaver as usual," as she gave her a squeeze on her arm.

"Hmmm. Interesting," said Abby

"What?" asked Peyton. Abby had scrunched her face with a quizzical look.

"It says he's not married. He's thirty years old, for Pete's sake. Wonder what that's all about?"

"Abby, it's really none of our business."

"Just curious Pey." It was obvious the wheels were in motion in Abby's head.

"Now Abby," pleaded Peyton, "please don't go prying." Peyton gave Abby a begging, exasperated look. She never knew what Abby would be up to next. Abby shrugged her shoulders with a glint in her eye.

What an imp, thought Peyton with a half grin.

Peyton couldn't help admire his chestnut brown, collar-length hair, thick and luxuriant. It was combed off his forehead, but any gust of wind could blow it down over his face. He was dressed casually with a crisply pressed brown and tan checked shirt with a tan V-neck sweater over it. A chocolate-brown sport jacket, khaki slacks and brown loafers completed the look. "What else does it say?" pressed Peyton.

"He's apparently a very smart cookie. He was chosen for this position over a lot of older, more well-known physicians. He apparently has outstanding expertise and is recognized for accomplishments in clone creation methods with flawless success."

"Well, we'll just see how smart he is. He is cute and fun to look at." Peyton still wasn't convinced this meeting of co-species was a good idea.

"Okay, deep breath, Peyton. They're coming in."

Little did Peyton know that this day would change her life, in fact, turn it upside down.

CHAPTER 4

Johann, still dumbstruck, walked to the front door as he continued to look around at the lush surroundings. Director of the International Clone Federation. Wow. But actually, he knew nothing about clones. His experience and knowledge focused on their creation, as well as overseeing the factories that produced them. Information about clone life was held in extreme secrecy, only known by a select few. So today was going to open up a whole new world for him. He felt humbled by the honor and privilege this appointment had bestowed on him

His father, also a physician, practiced in a New Hampshire community as a very successful heart surgeon. His mother, a CPA, had secretly hoped Johann would follow in her footsteps and join her in her prestigious, international firm. His sister practiced law and his brother chose medicine in pediatric intensive care. Swedish dad, Spanish mom. With this genetic combination, naturally all the siblings were stunning.

His brother and sister were both blond, blue-eyed, while Johann was dark- haired, with medium tanned skin and those unusual piercing blue eyes with black lashes and brows. His face was chiseled like a Norwegian nomadic god, but the smoldering look belied his Scandinavian heritage.

He was trim and fit, but only because he grudgingly worked out at a gym on orders from Kirt. He also ran when he could. Kirt made sure he did not overindulge on juicy hamburgers, which he loved.

So here he was now, joining the President of the New World Order and representatives of Europe and South America. This tour was of the utmost importance, as it would showcase the best clone community for world leaders to emulate in their own countries. He would be giving lectures worldwide using the United States' communities as the gold standard and would oversee the implementation of the clone lifestyles. He also would continue to visit clone creation factories to ensure that their quality and techniques were updated to the newest, highest standards. A big job, for sure, but he had a handpicked team in place that would be going ahead of him to assure compliance.

He approached the door as it swung open. When he saw her, his heart almost stopped. She was stunning in a gray, tight, sleeveless dress, with a large dark brown belt showing off her tiny waist. The dress stopped just above her knees, displaying her long, tanned legs. Her shoes, soft gray wedges, added at least three inches to her height. She wore a simple necklace, a gold strand with a large stone of grays and browns, a perfect accent to a simple but alluring dress. Gold earrings shone out from under her glistening hair.

Peyton extended her slender, perfectly manicured hand to welcome him. He felt an instant stirring like electricity shooting through his body. It struck him by surprise, and he let go and stepped back, still fixed on her beautiful dark eyes. He shook his head and brought himself back to the moment. Peyton, likewise, felt an unexplained inner desire that was confusing yet intriguing.

Abby stepped in and introduced herself and Peyton to Johann. "We are so pleased to meet you, Dr. Christiansen."

Struggling to recover from this unexpected shock, Peyton added, "I'm so delighted to introduce you to our world. I'm sure you will be pleased with all you see today. This tour is quite extensive, so let's gather in the boardroom where we will present an overview." She smiled broadly at this human with the indescribable blue eyes that threatened to melt her on the spot. She felt her cheeks burning, afraid they were probably giving off a brilliant, red glow.

"We'll make all the introductions there," said Abby, as she cut in, noticing the stunned look on Peyton's face. "Follow me," as she turned her head and glared at Peyton, motioning her to follow them.

Peyton drifted back instead. She had an uneasiness come over her again. She never felt her destiny would be like the other clones, but never quite knew why. She never, ever discussed this with anyone, not even her best friend and sister, Abby. She just always felt different.

For one thing, at twenty-eight now, Peyton had been seeing small changes in her face since age twenty, which certainly was not normal for clones. Clones never aged beyond twenty. Could this be possible? Very slight, but nonetheless, the signs were there- small lines extending out from her eyes. Luckily, no one had noticed them. She had been more concerned over the last year about how she could hide this oddity as time went on. She did not dwell on this subject often, but for some reason, this meeting had stirred the thought. "I am a happy, accomplished person living a very busy, enchanted life," she told herself. "I'm a highly educated clone with a master's degree in Information Science and an additional master's in Information Technology. I have no reason to be questioning anything. Why do these stupid issues keep creeping into my thoughts? Am I just imagining that I am aging in small ways? Am I becoming neurotic or psychotic?"

It was true that she did have a happy life and gave her all to everything she did. Her education had afforded skills to obtain information at the touch of her fingers. She could find any info in a matter of minutes. She explored a plethora of subjects and science questions that had plagued her. She had almost become an expert herself in the theory and process of cloning, following experts in the field from all over the world and studying their updates with rapt interest. Speaking of which, nowhere in the literature had any clone exhibited aging after their twentieth year. Maybe she just had a vivid imagination, and what she perceived as aging was nothing at all.

But how could she deny those feelings, the inner feelings so inexplicable? A desire of… she could not even find the words. She felt it again when she held the hand of that human. Never had she heard of a clone expressing any such feelings or had she ever seen it in all her research.

Well, I am totally fulfilled and happy with my wonderful life, she protested to herself. She was not going to think of this another second, and took off toward the boardroom, trailing the last of the group.

As Abby led the pack to the boardroom, she became very aware of the tall, handsome guy walking beside Dr. Christiansen. She noted they were chatting casually as they made their way into the room. Sure wish I were a human, she lamented to herself. What a hunk, using that decades old expression which had never gone out of vogue but very unclone-like. She suddenly remembered his picture from her prep book. She quickly realized he was the president of the New World Order.

Abby was striking in her dazzling daffodil yellow A line sheath with cap sleeves and round low neckline. The skirt fell to just above her knees. Her Manolo Blahnik four-inch heels showed off her well developed calves, a result from all her running. She and Peyton participated in marathons, when time allowed. They maybe were not the fastest but at least they always finished the race. Typically, just to stay in shape, they ran about fifteen miles a week. Her radiant white blond hair, now up in three tier buns, accentuated her entire face, with only a few tendrils falling past her cheekbones.

Miguel Tavares suddenly looked over and was captivated immediately by this adorable, perky clone who not only was gorgeous but also just happened to be the administrator of this entire community. Johann and Miguel looked at each other and smiled broadly.

Miguel whispered to Johann, "I suspect this is going to be an amazing day." He winked at Johann giving him a thumbs up.

CHAPTER 5

As the representatives congregated, partaking of the exquisite buffet, Abby and Peyton milled around, greeting everyone individually. This was a monumental moment for their community. The room oozed with excitement as the chatter rose to a dull roar.

"Okay, Peyton, you go talk to the President of the New World Order and I'll approach the sweet young doctor."

Peyton shot Abby an exaggerated look of impatience. She still felt very uneasy about this whole thing. "Abby, I can't wait till this day is over, even though I know this may be a great benefit for the people in our community. We've been the chosen one for the entire world to see, so I'm told. I guess I should be more impressed." She sighed, rolling her eyes. "But if this is really that important, I suppose I can tolerate the inconvenience in my life."

"I know you hate having the spot light on us, Peyton, but maybe this will really be to our advantage to get some things we are lacking." She could not really complain as their community pretty much had all they needed. They were not ones to ask for handouts, but keeping up to the minute with the latest in modern day technology would not hurt. She shook her finger at Peyton like a mother chastising her youngster. "Besides, my understanding is that they are choosing us to travel to other communities to offer our expertise. Peyton, this is an opportunity of a lifetime! And you know," laughing, "that is a long, long time."

"We'll give them another twenty minutes to eat and chat, and then we will start the program." Abby continued, "Get over to that hunk now and report back. I want every minute detail, too," she giggled. Abby gave Peyton a small shove in the direction of Miguel.

President Miguel Tavares was a hunk indeed. He was tall, 6'3," ruggedly handsome, dark complexion with black, very thick, wavy hair on the long side. He had dark eyes with accompanying dark, long lashes and visible facial hair that was impossible to shave off, leaving a perpetual, noticeable five o'clock shadow. Impeccably dressed, he wore khaki slacks with a light gray, V-neck sweater and a gray tweed sport jacket. He looked relaxed and comfortable in his casual attire. The saddle-brown, leather boots just added to his sexy image.

Reluctantly, Peyton made her way over and greeted him amicably, with her arm outstretched. He took her hand, pulled her to him, and kissed her warmly, first one cheek and then the other. Noticing her sudden stiffness he said. "Is customary in my homeland to kiss a beautiful senorita on both cheeks."

She blushed, as she was not used to this interesting way of greeting. Clones do hug and kiss, but it is like a mother to her child, or a brother to his sister. This certainly felt way different.

He took both her hands in his, prolonging her discomfort even more. "I am so looking forward to our tour today, and I know that this community will be the model for upgrading all the communities the world over. It appears you have a wonderful leader in Ms. Abigail, as I am learning. How fortunate," he continued, "this community is, to have you both advancing the lifestyle and happiness of all its citizens. Seeing all this for the first time, we are in awe."

An interesting concept, Peyton said to herself. Citizens. I guess I would not have used that exact term as I thought only humans were considered citizens of the United States. But then what are we? Hmmm. Well, we are our own segment of society. Peyton's head was spinning as she was still recovering from the double kiss and struggling to comprehend all that the president was saying in his thick, Spanish accent.

"I love our people, Mr. President, and their education and well-being are my life's purpose. And their life purpose is to live healthy, happily and to one day provide parts for their original humans. That is our destiny and we are more than excited to fulfill it."

"Well, we are very grateful for our clones," Miguel responded. As he was talking, he glanced at the swirl of yellow popping in and out of the crowd. He was so taken by that little, vivacious, powerful girl, Abby.

"Well, once again, Mr. President, we are just so delighted that you came to visit us and hope you will enjoy the tour we have planned. Please feel free to ask questions at any time. Abby and I will try to answer everything as best we can."

"Oh, I think I will have questions, alright," he said, as he let go of one of Peyton's hands, but lifted the other one up to his lips and kissed it softly. Peyton stared into his eyes trying to understand this warm gesture.

Peyton smiled meekly, turned and started to make her way through the crowd back to Abby. Abruptly, she came face to face with Johann as he suddenly turned around. Again that feeling overcame her like a lightning bolt. They locked eyes, and pulling away from the trance was almost next to impossible, but somehow she managed to speak. "Did you have enough to eat, Dr. Christiansen?" Peyton asked, attempting to make small talk.

"I did. It was all so very good too. I must ask though. I saw cows in your beautiful, serene pasture, yet I understood that clones do not eat meat or drink milk. Am I missing something here?"

She laughed, "Ah, we just love animals-all animals. We want our families and children to see these beautiful creatures, along with horses, donkeys and other four- legged critters. We have dogs, too, but don't eat them either." They both burst into laughter, still spellbound, staring into each other's eyes.

"But I just had a chicken salad, which incidentally, was beyond fantastic." He cocked his head with a dubious look on his face. He put both hands in the air and started laughing. Peyton laughed hysterically, watching him realize that it was not chicken.

"I must stop this or I won't have any mascara left on my lashes." She blotted her tears, with a napkin she grabbed from the table.

"I'm not sure you need mascara with your lovely lashes," he said.

Peyton blushed, an odd feeling for her. He was just so incredibly enticing. She was not sure how to take the compliment. It stirred up unexplainable emotions. "Well, if you will excuse me, I am sure Abby is pacing by now waiting for me to get up there." She pulled away, but felt his eyes follow her every step to the front of the room. She had conquered her nervousness, but now she was becoming very self-conscious.

Abby moved to the podium and brought the room to a complete

silence. Her superb education with multiple degrees in business management had prepared her well. The minute she started addressing the group, her beauty became incidental to her intellect. Well almost.

"If I could have your attention, please. On behalf of Peyton, our entire staff, and myself, I welcome you all to our lovely community. To give you a little background, I will start with a historical overview of our area.

"My name is Abigail, otherwise known as Abby. I am the administrator of this wonderful community. My cohort, next to me, is Peyton, who is the administrator of the educational system. As an aside, we are sisters." She threw her arms around Peyton and drew her close. "I know, like day and night." The crowd roared. "But we grew up in the same house and had the same wonderful parents." Peyton squirmed away with an expression of discomfort. Once again, Abby was being Abby, zany Abby. She started to giggle with the crowd.

"As you have seen while driving up to our gates, this area of New York State is one of the most beautiful in the entire state. Sorry for hogging it." Again, everyone laughed.

Miguel was especially rapt in listening to her. He was mesmerized by her. He glanced around the room and saw everyone also fixed on this little creature in yellow. Johann bumped Miguel's leg repeatedly with his foot, making him smile even more.

"We have so much to be thankful for, having been assigned to this particular area of the state. It not only is scenically beautiful, but very fertile and ideal for growing all the fruits, vegetables, and grains that are our mainstay. It originally was made up of Chenango, Otsego and Delaware counties. We also have a smidgen of Broom County, including Oquaga Creek State Park." Abby was beaming.

Miguel leaned over and whispered to Johann. "Dios Mio! Is such a shame clones don't have the capacity to feel romantic love and desire as we humans. Now why was that genetically engineered out of them, por favor?"

Johann smiled sheepishly. "It didn't make sense for clones to fall in love, let alone make love. Remember, their whole purpose is to supply parts for us guys. They cannot propagate their species. We make them from a test tube. Remember, amigo?"

Abby chattered on, "We are two hundred and fifty square miles, so we have the beautiful mountains of the Catskills as well as the rolling foothills. Lakes and creeks are plentiful. The little hamlets like Oxford and Norwich are basically still there. Oneonta, with its rich Iroquois Indian heritage, is virtually intact too. It was originally named for its table rocks, a prominent geological formation at the western end of the city, and they are still there to this day. It was also home to the State University of New York at Oneonta and Hartwick College. They are there, but the buildings, of course, have been completely renovated."

No one seemed to mind the long and involved history she was reporting, as they seemed to just enjoy her presence and enthusiasm. She continued, "Algonquin and Iroquois Indians originally inhabited the land around the city of Oneonta, but the Iroquois gained exclusive control during the early historic period. The first pioneers arrived around 1775 and consisted mainly of Palatine Germans and Dutch settlers moving out of the Hudson Valley. The first hamlet appeared around 1800 and was later known as Milfordville. Its name changed to Oneonta in 1832, and it eventually incorporated as a village."

Abby loved to talk about the history, using her hands in wide movements to accentuate her talk. "God, she's cute," whispered Miguel to Johann. "Can you smart scientific guys maybe undo what you did to them?"

"You wish, big guy. I can't take my eyes off Peyton. I have never seen a more beautiful specimen in my whole life. I still can't believe they're not original humans. They're good imitations. If I figure out how to change them, I'll let you know," he said facetiously, throwing Miguel a punch in his arm.

"When the Delaware and Hudson Railroad reached Oneonta, the village began a growth spurt and once was home to the largest locomotive roundhouse in the world. Oneonta, like the rest of the towns and villages in this geographical location, has not changed that much over the last seventy-five years. We are very proud to be part of the evolution of this area and feel it is our responsibility to maintain its beauty and value. We take pride in being the keepers of villages and vast land that once was human territory."

Abby continued to expound on the history of Community 27 and the standards of excellence they had achieved in education and science as well as in production of goods and services. Everyone could see how proud she was of their accomplishments.

For such a little thing, she had a very commanding way about her.

She was authoritative and had the respect of everyone within the community. And she demanded excellence. Her need for perfection was very evident. Her prowess helped her to attain it.

Peyton then came forward and added, "Much effort and funding have been contributed to assure that clone lives are comfortable, rewarding, and progressive in all aspects. You just didn't know it. We couldn't be more grateful to the humans for their continuing support. We are proud to report that we are now, for the most part, self supporting."

Johann leaned over and said to Miguel. "Remember, The Clone Federation, domestic and international had full approval to acquire lands where they thought fit. Humans were relocated from chosen lands and provided with new homes in new areas of their choice. Eminent domain was not a topic of dissent with humans. If their homes and properties were selected, they left without question or argument. Their small sacrifice paled in comparison to having their very own clone, a genetic copy, to prolong their life." Miguel nodded in agreement.

"But we did not know they lived like this. I, myself, just thought they were robot- like, living in confined spaces like cattle. I knew we gave them land, but thought that was for hiding them from society, so there would be no contact. After all, they were just body parts." The enormity of the reality was sinking in as Miguel shook his head, almost ashamed of what the scientific community had done. He looked back to the podium, now with reverence.

"Today we will be traveling around to give you a comprehensive view of our lifestyle." Peyton finished by saying, "Thank you all again for coming to visit us. This is a historic event. We are looking forward to assisting you in other communities or otherwise be available in an advisory capacity."

Everyone clapped and stood up from their chairs to come forward to shake hands with Abby and Peyton and make their acquaintance. They could hardly wait for the tour to start, especially Miguel and Johann. They were very eager to spend more time with these two dynamos.

CHAPTER 6

Everyone filed out of the room, all anticipating the next part of the program. First they toured the library-education facility. The technological sophistication totally astounded Johann. Computer terminals occupied most of the area, and large screens for student presentations covered the walls. The enormity of it all was unbelievable. They had information at their fingertips with the ability to bring it up instantaneously. Students carried Kindles on which to download info. No book in sight. But charger stations appeared everywhere.

"Come out this way," Peyton said, gesturing toward the back of the building. They followed her outside to find a vast expanse of gardens and walkways. Small alcoves with numerous benches, presumably for outdoor classes or hanging out, surrounded the pathways off the main corridor. Everything was conducive to a relaxed atmosphere for positive learning.

Peyton was pointing out the minute details of the area. "Here we have a spot for getting smoothies, hot green tea or vegetarian snacks of all kinds. Students seem to have an endless appetite."

Johann replied, "My medical school days certainly weren't like this."

Miguel added, "We were stuffed into lecture halls with five hundred-plus students. We had the high technology, of course, but no creature comforts."

Johann's jaw dropped open. "Who would have known they had advanced technology on par with us?"

There were students passing by, going in various directions. Johann could not help but think, "They are exactly like us, but they are not like us." He had to keep reminding himself of the difference. Even knowing the reason for their existence, it was hard to actually see them in the flesh and understand their acceptance of their fate. Their good nature was such a refreshing respite from the real world. Why couldn't humans be more like them? Johann thought. But then they are created to have this personality. It does not come naturally. It had taken years to perfect it too. But as he was contemplating this, another thought came to him. That Peyton does not exactly display this trait. He could not really put his finger on it, but there was something different about her. He had not even talked to her that much yet. There was just that inflection in her voice. And she appeared annoyed when she thought no one was paying attention.

They viewed a high school and elementary school that were within walking distance, a bit of a hike. Abby was able to keep up in her little spike heels, which continually impressed Miguel. Peyton, on the other hand, had more sensible heels, tall, but wider. They all congregated back at the library where a large electric multi-person bus waited at the front entrance.

"Now for the rolling tour," announced Abby. She grabbed Miguel, Johann and Kirt and stated, "You can get on last and sit up front with Peyton and me so we can point out important landmarks and pertinent sites." They certainly were okay with that.

After everyone was seated, the silent vehicle pulled away. The electric vehicle, now prevalent in all societies, was such a boom to the ecology; it totally eradicated pollution from emissions that had plagued the world for so many years.

Johann and Miguel sat together across from Abby and Peyton in the front row. They had a fantastic view from the front and the sides. Windows were everywhere, even in the ceiling. Johann said, "Abby and Peyton, we can't thank you enough for the courtesy you have extended to us. I know this event is out of the realm of normal for you, and you have handled it graciously." Peyton, now tongue-tied, nodded as Abby spoke.

"We have done much preparation for your visit and are happy we could do it. Actually, there has been some opposition among our people about your impending visit, but in the end, we all came together in total agreement. We know it is necessary to improve conditions for other communities and that this is, in fact, a top secret expedition, not to be shared with humans other than those directly involved in this project."

"We can assure you that this visit is classified and all have been cleared through the International Intelligence Agency. Not to worry," explained Miguel. He could understand their reluctance to receive these humans, and not wanting to contaminate their society. He hoped this visit would dispel any idea that harm would come to them. His eyes met Abby's beautiful blue ones and he smiled reassuringly. She looked away, shyly, afraid of the feelings she was having toward a human. He, in turn, couldn't stop looking at her.

They were passing by the extensive pastures now with a closer look at their pet cows. Johann chuckled when he saw them. There were little goats too. "Hmmm, all that goat milk going to waste," he said under his breath.

Just then, Miguel whispered to him. "In Brazil, goats make a delicious tasty tapas, especially with goat cheese on top."

Johann smirked at him. "Well, you know, these people aren't dying of heart disease or strokes, so maybe we should take a lesson from them. Maybe we wouldn't have needed replacement clones in the first place."

Miguel countered, "Yeah, but what fun are they having? No whole pigs roasting over an open fire. That's an old tradition that is still done in my country to this day. It's like an event, an entire day revolves around a juicy, roasting pig. Lots of alcohol consumed too, of course. Yum mojitos. And the dancing and singing," he continued. "It's an event, I tell you." He had a heavy Spanish accent, but the more he talked about his heritage, the heavier it got. He would even revert to Spanish when describing his country. Being Brazilian, he also spoke Portuguese. But he spent so much time in Spain growing up, he preferred Spanish.

"Well, an event for this northeasterner would be the same pig, but cut into chops and barbecued over an open gas grill on the backyard patio. Also alcohol consumption, but not sure about the mojitos. In nice weather, this event would revolve around one's swimming pool and also have loud music. Just not salsa." They both laughed. "Of course, in my youth, most of my summers were spent in Sweden," said Johann. A lot of outdoor activities, yachting with Kirt, chasing young girls and eating wonderful Swedish dishes.

Kirt piped in from the seat behind them. "Aye, those were the days. We managed to survive too." He punched the back of Johann's seat. "Course Joey here almost got me killed many a time," he said, laughing as he recalled their boyhood days.

Abby and Peyton sat listening, envious. They had never ventured out past their walls to see any other way of life. They were aware of other standards of living as they were Internet savvy and discussed it quite a lot with each other, secretly, though. Clones would have absolutely no interest in going anywhere past their walls. To actually hear about it from human lips for the first time was extraordinary. They looked at each other wistfully.

They were now going through villages and hamlets that Abby had spoken of. They were not going to be able to even see a fifth of it due to time constraints. But Peyton hoped she had picked out a good representation. They saw storage areas with gigantic refrigerated and freezer units for stockpiling the food supply, mostly grown within their borders. There were abundant grocery stores to supply the four million people who populated the community. Their produce was shared with other communities as needed too, all of it being grown organically, using no pesticides or fertilizer. They went past hybrid almond trees, walnut trees and at least forty varieties of apple trees. The maples had cans on them to catch the natural sap dripping out of the trees. There also were a huge variety of greens, arugula, spinach, and kale to lettuces of every kind.

Peyton explained, "We also grow all kinds of root vegetables that are very high in protein and nutrients."

Johann could not believe the extensiveness of their agriculture. And a lot of the vegetables he had not even heard of. "I guess being a vegetarian, you have to be pretty creative," he said, his eyes wide with wonderment.

They arrived at Oneonta and had a quick drive by the old office buildings that were still intact. They also circled the colleges up the hill. On the outskirts, in contrast, there was an abundance of shopping areas, gym and health centers, and tons of restaurants, all vegetarian, of course. That being said, they still had individual cuisine. There was an Asian restaurant, a barbecue shack, a German Wursthaus and the run-of-the- mill fast food joints. The border was just short of Cooperstown. There was no way the humans were going to give up their Baseball Hall of Fame town with hundreds of years of legend. But they had Milford, a tiny village eight miles from Cooperstown that had hundreds of years of its own history. They looped around and headed back to the library facility where they had started.

The entire tour was breathtaking. Witnessing their advancement and self-containment overwhelmed the humans. They were surprised to see cars, all electric, most without drivers at the wheel, traveling to destinations simply from data-entry commands. They had these in the human world too but it was a surprise to see the clone community with this advancement. They pulled up to the library building where they departed the MPV.

Peyton spoke up first. "Did you gentlemen enjoy the tour? Or did we bore you to death?" She had a knowing twinkle in her eye, as she was well aware they were totally astonished. They had that look of disbelief the entire time.

Johann stuttered. "Ah, sure was not what I was expecting. And I'm supposed to be an expert on clone creation."

Miguel showed equal amazement. "I am envious of your world. There seems to be so much accomplishment here as well as contentment. I don't see evidence of competitiveness or jealousy anywhere."

They all walked together through the massive doorway and into the boardroom where they had started. Awaiting them was a wonderfully prepared dinner in a lavish setting.

"My goodness," said Johann, his mouth dropping open. "It looks wonderful."

The room had been transformed into a beautiful, formal dining room with white tablecloths, fresh flowers adorning each table and exquisite bone china with crystal goblets and wine glasses. The lighting was low with an ambience of a very romantic French chalet.

By now Kirt was entranced with it all. He had been on the heels of these two guys constantly and had said nothing for four hours. But now he had to let it out. "I think I could be totally comfortable here. Do you mind if I quit my job, boss, and just stay here? Sex be damned, I'd adjust." His flyaway, blond hair was in disarray as usual and he actually looked like he would fit right in with this lifestyle-except for the non-competitive part. He'd been competitive his entire life. They all roared with laughter.

Just then Peyton walked up. "Okeydokey, you guys, what's the joke? I think I will have to separate you three at dinner." And she did. She placed Johann next to her, Miguel next to Abby and Kirt next to London, a lovely assistant with ravishing red hair.

Kirt smiled from ear to ear. "Like I said," he blurted out.

The main course was thick-sliced, what appeared to be beef with a rich, seasoned sauce over the top. It was garnished with fresh herbs. Fresh, steamed zucchini, yellow squash and kale accompanied it with whole-wheat rice and quinoa. The taste was indescribable. Goblets were filled with ice cold, best-tasting water on earth. Crusty bread was served on the side with Earth Balance spread, a non-animal-fat butter. The dark red wine, from grapes grown in their own vineyard, was robust and delicious.

As the men devoured their meal, the gals chatted endlessly. Peyton was telling of the new baby that just arrived at their home, with Abby adding her perspective of its cuteness. Johann, so captivated by the conversation and caught up in the atmosphere, did not want this evening to end.

Abby finally said, "I hope you all enjoyed your day and can go home and reflect on what you saw and learned today." She thought to herself, I sound like an old formal schoolteacher. She actually wanted to say, "So, did we impress you humans so you can actually learn how to live life the correct way? No crime, obesity, and hateful murders…" she could go on and on.

Peyton continued, "When you are ready for Abby and me to help with your international ventures, let us know. I expect you are anxious to improve communities all over the world and maybe want to develop a plan to replicate our advanced community. I believe I am already scheduled to travel to other U.S. clone communities to assess the education and library programs. We will be implementing updated models of learning as a start."

Johann said, "You cannot even imagine what impact you have made on me, ahhh, on our leaders here today. My staff now has a lot of work ahead of them to convert this model into workable plans for other communities." He just realized his heart was beating out of his chest.

Miguel piped in "My friend here will be working night and day, I can assure you, as he does not just shuck it off to his staffers. He is a workaholic and a perfectionist."

"Nah," responded Johann. "I am just a figurehead." Kirt retorted, "Sure, Joey, and like I don't have to constantly force you to get the heck off your computer and get to bed."

"Well, what else do I have to do, besides going to boring dinners and honorary awards benefits that I am obligated to attend.

Peyton, remembering that there was no wife in the picture, now had the distinct impression that there was no significant other in his life either. She thought that was rather strange as she gathered that most men of his prominence had to have a trophy wife at their side. Very interesting for sure.

Johann said, "I probably will need to frequently touch base with you, Peyton, in fact both of you, actually. I hope that's ok with you both."

Peyton's head was starting to swirl, "Of course, no problem." So there would be more contact. She was hoping, but on the other hand, dreading.

Abby lit up and said, "Mr. President, you are also welcome to return anytime."

He grinned, "I am sure that will be necessary, senorita."

Abby was so taken with his wide smile and dimples. And those, dark, smoldering eyes. She looked even smaller standing next to him.

They all actually hated to see the evening wind down. But it was getting late and there was a four-hour drive ahead of them, so end it they must. They all said their good-byes with polite kisses and lots of handshaking all around.

As Johann was getting into his car, he waved to Peyton. Once again she felt that overwhelming wave of desire. It was getting harder and harder to shake it off.

Miguel walked to his own awaiting car and shouted, "Talk to you soon, Johann. Safe travels," and disappeared into the black, tinted-windowed SUV. There were four other SUVs surrounding it as they pulled out in a caravan.

Kirt decided to ride back with Johann to go over his schedule for the next few exhausting days of non-stop meetings. Johann said to him, "Kirt, I really had no idea how this visit was going to affect me. Their community is incredible."

"I know," he replied, "who would have guessed?" shaking his head

"And that Peyton, there's just something about her," Johann continued.

Kirt interrupted. "My friend, you know she is totally off limits. How could you even consider thinking what I know you're thinking? Are you nuts?"

"I know, I know," he countered, "but…" his thoughts drifting off.

"No buts, Joey. Let me ask you this: If she is so dynamic, albeit, missing a few essential items, just what do you think her original human would be like? She is exactly the same, buddy. Now doesn't it make more sense to go after her? The exact same girl!!!" He was shouting now.

As if a light bulb came on, "Kirt, you are perfectly correct. You're a genius. I could have Peyton, only as a human counterpart with all the really, really essential parts. I must start looking for her immediately. Cancel my meetings for the next four days," he commanded.

"Whoa, lover boy. Are you crazy? To go looking for a babe right now? We have some very important negotiations that I think take precedence over your love life."

"Kirt," he pleaded, "I have to find her. I must find her. I can't wait."

Kirt just groaned, "Oh you fool. OK, but just four days. You hear me? You have just four days," hitting him on his head with his papers.

The search began.

CHAPTER 7

There was no sense pleading with Johann at this point. He had his mind made up. Kirt gave up and gave in to his insane buddy.

Just then Johann's cell phone rang. "Hey, Mom! Yeah, I am on my way home. Went great. I know, you poor original humans have no idea about clone life, but that's the way it's going to stay. No, I'm not telling you just because you're my mother." He rolled his eyes to Kirt.

"How's dad? Good." As he heard the next familiar question he groaned. Kirt looked at him, knowingly. "No, mom, Kirt and I are not dating anyone seriously. Mom, we are working hard day and night. Of course, you will be the first to know." Kirt winked at him.

"Bye, Mom; oh, Kirt says hi. Love you too."

As he hung up, Kirt burst into laughter. "Your mom is so anxious for us to find our soul mates. She wants to ruin all our fun."

"I know, but then we are getting old Kirt. Thirty and thirty-two are considered prime marriage age," he shot back. He scrunched his forehead in fake worry. He kicked off his boots, lowered the back of his seat and stretched out, giving a big yawn. "Well, we'll see what happens when I meet Ms. Peyton's original human. If I am so unbelievably drawn to Peyton, can you just imagine what it's going to be like with her OH? Adding emotional and physical love to the equation---I can't even fathom." Johann was grinning ear to ear. "I have not even had a real date in…wow has it been over a year? Pretty pathetic for a young stud like me," he said, staring at nothing, shaking his head.

"Okay, Joey, but slow down. This human may not be exactly like her clone. Besides, she's probably married; did you ever think of that?"

How could he put some sense into this lovesick maniac?

"Ahhh yeah, kind of, but I was not going to let that stop me," he laughed, focusing on Kirt with stubborn determination.

"Well, her husband may stop you, you idiot."

"Hmmm, maybe. But the first thing I have to do is find her. Luckily, being the top guy, I have the ability to peruse the data bank and bring up her info: Name, whereabouts, and other personal data. Lucky me!"

"You are a privileged dude. I'll help you, against my better judgment, though. I don't want you getting your ass killed," Kirt said, relenting.

"Thank you, bro."

As the car weaved through the hills and valleys back to New York City, Johann closed his eyes to catch a quick catnap. Kirt followed suit as all the arranging and prep work wiped him out. As Kirt was drifting off, his mind briefly recalled that blazing redheaded clone. Damn, he was thinking, sure would love to see that London again. Who knew these clones would be so damn hot? What a waste.

The next day Johann was up at his usual 5:00 am. He downed a half-cup of coffee and headed out the door to do a three-mile run in Central Park. Not surprisingly, he passed other diehards getting their exercise in before the day got in the way. It was still technically summer, the last week of August, but already getting crisp early in the mornings, cool enough to pull the hoody up over his head.

He had finished his run and jumped in the shower, hurrying so he could get to his computer. He was really eager to start his search for Peyton's OH.

Kirt came strolling out of his room, half asleep. "Hey, Joey, why didn't you wake me? I would have run with you," although to look at him you would have thought he was lying. His hair was sticking out on all sides and his eyes were like slits, barely open.

"Nah, old man. You were out cold and needed the extra hour sleep," he chided him.

"Well, I was coherent enough this morning to call Sammy. She will change all our appointments. But only four days, buddy boy. Not that I want to stand in the way of love, but hey, we do have work to do.

Unless you have forgotten who you are."

"Yeah, yeah, thanks. Let's just get this done, Kirt.

Johann plopped down at his computer and brought up the Clone Federation Registry and entered a number. Within seconds, up popped Peyton's info: date, place of birth, community number and a plethora of other information. He then looked up the corresponding Human ID. Bingo. Here it was. Name: Caitlyn Sarantino, age twenty-eight. Many addresses, among them, New York City. Occupation: CEO/Owner, Caitlyn Couture.

Wow, one of the most prestigious fashion houses in New York, let alone the world. His mind was spinning. Married three years, now divorced.

"OK Kirt. Now you don't have to worry about my knees being busted," he announced. A slow smile of relief spread across his face.

Next he brought up a current picture, in fact, a slew of pictures. "Hmmm, quite the social butterfly," quipped Kirt. He pushed Johann over to get a better look.

"Holy moly," shouted Johann. "She is a bombshell." He raised his hand to Kirt for a high five, and then unable to contain himself, started bouncing up and down in his chair.

"Would you calm down? Geez, you're like a goofy middle schooler. Let's plan our strategy," said Kirt. "You can't just show up on her doorstep and explain your lust for her because of your lust for Peyton."

"Um, you're right. Okay, how about I call her about meeting her to order an outfit for my mom for a, ahhh, a gala?"

"Okay, good. Go for it." Kirt was rubbing his hands together finally getting a little more excited, but at the same time, trying to keep Johann at an even keel.

"Are you going to go with me?" asked Johann, "or would that look weird?"

"A little awkward. You're on your own, my friend."

Johann had a few business calls to make to get everything out of the way so hopefully no one would bother him for a few days. It was now 1:00 pm. Time to make his call. His hands were clammy, and beads of sweat developed on his forehead. His heart started to race. Calm down, he told himself. He dialed the number.

"Caitlyn Couture," a friendly voice announced on the other end.

"I would like to speak with Ms. Caitlyn Sarantino, please."

"She's not available at this moment, but I will connect you with Ms. Christine Clark. Please hold."

Johann could hear his voice cracking, so cleared his throat before Christine picked up. I have to have my story ready, he nervously thought to himself when another equally pleasant voice came on.

"This is Christine Clark. May I help you?" she asked. She clearly had a British accent.

"I, ahhh, would like to talk with Ms. Sarantino about a gown for my mother," he stammered. "I would prefer to talk directly with Ms. Sarantino, if that's okay." Johann was frantically thinking of a possible gala coming up to refer to. His mind was blank.

Knowing direct personal calls were never acceptable to Caitlyn, except for a few choice clients, Christine countered, "I will be more than happy to give her the message, Mr.... I did not get your name."

"Dr. Johann Christiansen," he said, listening to see if she recognized his famous name. Apparently she did not, as she continued.

"I will be happy to give her the message as soon as she contacts me. I am not expecting her in today. She has a tight schedule," she lied while thinking, she's probably home nursing a hangover from the latest party or hanging out with her spoiled, lazy girlfriends.

"Thank you for your courtesy," he replied. He hung up actually relieved she was not there. He felt so unprepared. But then, postponing it may be even worse. His palms were even clammier as he grabbed a towel to wipe them. Well, now I have time to get even more anxious, he whined to himself. I hope I can keep up this ruse after I meet her.

Since he left his cell number, he decided to strap his phone on his belt and head down to the gym to alleviate his nervousness with a good workout.

He had finished his second shower for the day when his cell phone rang. He looked at the number, and it was Caitlyn Couture.

Oh man, he sighed. I'm going to sound like an idiot, I'm sure. He took a deep breath, remembered the reason he was embarking on this crazy adventure, and visualized Caitlyn from the pictures.

Kirt had left a long time ago, so he was truly on his own. He reached for the phone.

CHAPTER 8

At sixteen she was an international model, reaching superstar status. Although her 5'6" frame would ordinarily disqualify her from that very competitive arena, her ravishing beauty flung her to stardom.

Now at twenty-eight she had elevated herself, becoming the creator of one of the most prestigious fashion houses in New York. Her haute couture rivaled the decades-old houses of Versace, Oscar de la Renta and Valentino. Caitlyn Couture created exclusive, custom-fitted clothing made from high-quality, expensive fabric. It was sewn with extreme attention to detail and finished by the most time-consuming, hand-executed techniques. Her client list included royalty from Europe and Scandinavia, as well as starlets, the well-heeled and business elite from around the world. The waiting list was endless, so some original designs were mass-produced for those who could not wait for individual fitting. Only upscale shops sold her designs.

But Caitlyn Sarantino had become bored with the constant demand of designing. Her well-chosen staff now did all the work. Best kept secret in the trade too. All Caitlyn did now was demand perfection, but contributed very little inspiration or design ideas.

She was becoming more and more depressed. New York gave her the constant spotlight, high society lifestyle and, of course, constant flow of guys to take home and bed on a regular basis. She was all about parties and traveling the world, seeking thrills and new romantic adventures. Although she owned a very successful business, thanks to her daddy who pay rolled the empire, she still felt something was missing. According to her, life just sucked.

Caitlyn was gorgeous with a well-toned, slim body, kept that way by two trainers on call twenty-four/seven and her favorite plastic surgeon, who sucked out fat anytime she spent too many months gorging on Italian or French food. Men were constantly pursuing her. But with all she had, she was miserable. Her marriage had been a monstrous failure. He was handsome, had high standing in social circles, but was a dreadful mamma's boy. He never met her expectations, and she dumped him after three years of extreme disappointment and total boredom. The final straw was when he wanted to start a family.

Maybe she just was incapable of loving anyone. She spent much of her time relieving her unhappiness with booze, men and pleasure drugs. Designer drugs were totally legal now and quite common on the celebrity scene. It did not really matter the damage it did to organs. They were replaceable, thanks to modern science. What a fantastic age to be living in, she often thought, without regard to what she was doing to her body.

Caitlyn was her usual unhappy, bitchy self today. No trips scheduled, so no one- night stands to look forward to in a romantic country. This really sucks, she moaned to herself. She might as well go to the office and see what designs were in the works, as she wriggled into one of her own dress designs, a light-beige, cashmere dress with a wide, black, leather belt. She added a short cropped, leather jacket to match her high black boots. She looked into a floor length mirror and stated, "I am just so stunning," and poofed her lips as if to kiss herself. Her hair was flowing down her shoulders, blond strands sparkling in the sunrays that streamed through her bedroom window. She applied a light-coral lipstick to her already perfect makeup that only accentuated her beauty, didn't hide it. Her naturally long, dark lashes were a striking contrast to her radiant blond hair. Her alluring, velvet-brown eyes, attributed to Italian descent from her father's side, were a trait that could transform the most adept person into a bumbling idiot. They were mesmerizing and she knew just how to use them. She could captivate anyone she wanted and learned very early how to do it. French traits from her mother's side contributed to her lithe body. She was probably one of the most beautiful women in the world, on par with Elizabeth Taylor from the twentieth century. Unfortunately, Caitlyn knew it and used it to get her way.

She hurriedly gulped down the last of her coffee and rushed out to the waiting town car that she had ordered fifteen minutes earlier.

"Hey, Caitlyn, where to?" asked Tom.

"The office, unfortunately," she said with a groan as Tom helped her into the back seat.

He smiled as he closed her door and got in behind the wheel. He had been driving her since she was very young, so knew this very self-centered, overindulged party girl very well. Daddy and Mommy each having their own active lives, pacified her by throwing more money her way to keep her from whining. Many times she had come to him with adolescent questions about boys and her current crisis in school. He loved her like his own daughter and worried about her constantly.

They arrived at the swank office building, rivaling the best and most expensive in New York City. Even the old Trump Building could not hold a candle to this magnificent, opulent architecture.

"Thanks, Tom," she said as he opened her door. "I'll call you when I'm ready to leave." Tom nodded with a smile. "Have a good day, sweetheart." He actually felt sorry for her. She just did not seem to enjoy her life, even with unlimited funds and opportunities at her disposal. She swung her legs out and bounced to her feet. Grabbing her $16,000 handbag, she threw him a wave and scurried off to the gold-lined entrance where the exquisitely uniformed doorman greeted her.

"Ms. Sarantino." He welcomed her with a smile and tip of his hat. She barely acknowledged him.

She entered her suite on the fifth floor with a snippy greeting. "Hi y'all. Are we earning our paychecks today?"

Her administrator, Couture Director, Christine, a very sharply dressed, forty-five-ish, stunning lady strode to her side, greeting her warmly. "Caitlyn, what a wonderful surprise. You look marvelous as always. How was France?"

"Same old, same old," she responded, revealing a hint of boredom in her voice.

"Well, come, let me show you what we're working on. The Princess Carolina needs a complete wardrobe for a royal visit to Asia and needs it in one month! We are scrambling to obtain all the material. The designers are working feverishly to come up with a haute couture line for her. Come see," Christine said, motioning Caitlyn to follow her.

Caitlyn waved an impatient hand toward Christine. "That's great, Christine, but I think I will work in my office for awhile. Any messages?"

"Here are a few from the last several days," responded Christine, not even disappointed in Caitlyn's non-interest in the project at hand. Typical Caitlyn.

Fashion Week, occurring over a six-week period, brought buyers from all over the world to capture new trends. The show taking place at Carrousel du Louvre, situated below the Louvre Museum, was reserved for fashion professionals, as well as celebrities and the rich and famous. Hairstylists, makeup artists and coordinators rushed around preparing the exquisite supermodels for their walk down the catwalks, to show off the latest designs of the most prominent fashion houses, including the French design houses of Celine, Commes des Garcons, Chanel and Lanvin. Each designer produced a runway show with its own elaborate theme that radiated artistic talent and creativity.

"Caitlyn," called Simone. "Have you met Juillet? She was just signed and is absolutely gorgeous."

"Oh really?" replied Caitlyn with raised eyebrows. Caitlyn held the top rank of the most beautiful and highest paid model in the world. She, now twenty years old, had reached the pinnacle in just four years. She traveled in high circles and was recognized the world over.

"Wait until you see her, Cait. She's working with us today."

"Is that so?" Caitlyn grabbed the lipstick out of makeup artist Carla's hand and threw it across the room. "You idiot," she screamed. "You're not putting that hideous color on me." Her mood was clearly going south, her ugly temper, once again, rising, which it often did at the most unpredictable of events.

"Simone, where did she come from and why is she working this show? No one usurps me." She pushed Carla away.

"I guess you haven't heard. She's the granddaughter of model Giselle Larchen who was world-renowned fifty years ago. Juillet is even more beautiful than she and only eighteen years old. You were sixteen when you started, right?"

"Yes," snapped Caitlyn. "So she's walking today for sure? Why was I not told about this?" Caitlyn hated competition and was used to being number one at Fashion Week. No one ever dared to show her up. "I will see about this. Carla, get me my agency on the phone immediately," she demanded.

"Ms. Sarantino, you are five minutes away from your entrance. I need to finish your makeup, and Anja needs to complete your ensemble."

"Screw you both. I said get my agent immediately." She grabbed a brush off the counter and threw it at Carla, hitting her on the side of her face. It would have hit her squarely in the nose had she not attempted to duck. Carla complied, dialed the number and handed the phone to Caitlyn.

"Michael, you moron. I thought you were looking out for my interests. What's this about Modi hiring some eighteen-year-old kid, and one with connections, I might add?"

Michael responded, "Caitlyn, relax. You know you are the star. No one can match your beauty and talent. You know modeling agencies have to have a variety of girls present, enough to showcase all the designer haute couture in the shows. You have nothing to worry about, baby. You are the best."

"Well, from what I hear, she is breathtaking," she barked into the phone.

"Caitlyn, I'm sure you two will be the best of friends in no time. Your concern is totally unfounded."

"It better be or your ass will be looking for another job and believe it, once I'm done with you, you will be relegated to representing B-list, has-been actors."

Caitlyn slammed the phone down. The stage director yelled, "Caitlyn, you're on in three minutes. Let's hustle, babe."

Carla and Anja did the best they could and pushed her to the entrance of the stage. "Go do your thing, Ms. Sarantino."

Caitlyn threw on her artificial facial expression and strutted out onto the stage to an outburst of applause. Her famous walk was televised throughout the world and she thrived on the adulation.

As she returned to the stage, she got a glimpse of the next model emerging from behind the curtain. Out came a gorgeous creature, much taller than she, with legs like a gazelle and luxuriant brown hair, falling in soft curls all the way to her hips. So this is the new nymph, Caitlyn cackled to herself. She felt intense jealousy and hatred deep within her core. This is not going to stand, she vowed. I'm Caitlyn Sarantino, and I will not be intimidated by this privileged copycat. I don't care who her granny is.

Juillet glided down the walkway to gasps and applause. Her lithe body oozed sexiness, and her smile lit up the room.

Caitlyn, peeking from behind the curtain, witnessed this sudden adoration of her rival. She pulled off her accessories and threw them in all directions. She then ripped off her very expensive outfit, leaving it on the floor, and stomped off. Everyone jumped out of her way as she headed toward her dressing room. No one dared go near her when she was in one of her funks. She disappeared into her room, slamming the door behind her.

The director rushed over to Carla. "OK, what's it going to take to coax her out of there to finish her gig?"

"Forget it, Beau. She's done for today. She's probably downing a bottle of Chateau Lafite Rothschild." Carla shrugged her shoulders.

Beau slapped his program clipboard against his leg in defeat and yelled, "OK, girlfriends, let's keep the flow going. Anja, get Caitlyn's apparel and put them on Juillet. She will do double duty. And make them fit!" He walked to the curtain and pulled it back to watch the processing of models. Juillet came around him and continued to the catwalk. Again the audience cheered and stood up, clapping. Beau gave a sigh of relief. He didn't need a pissed designer. Caitlyn's disappearance was hardly noticed.

The following day, Caitlyn arrived with her entourage, her mood decisively improved.

"Good morning, all," she said with an actual smile on her face.

Carla and Anja descended on her to get her ready for the catwalk. They had forty-five minutes to do her makeup and hair and put her look together. Caitlyn continued to be civil and had no throwing incident. Carla and Anja collectively gave a sigh of relief.

Caitlyn glanced to her right and noticed her nemesis sitting at a makeup station five chairs away. Her mood deteriorated as she felt a burning in her face, and her heartbeat pick up speed. Suddenly she smiled and called down the line, "Hello, ladies. Let's go wow them again today." They all waved back to Caitlyn, but no one wanted to engage in conversation with her.

Beau came bouncing in. "Five minutes, ladies. Time to line up and prepare to amaze." He loved Fashion Week. Where else could he be around drop-dead gorgeous babes? They were to come out from both sides of the stage, then alternate one by one down the runway. There would be one going and one coming on the catwalk at all times.

Caitlyn and Juillet were on opposite sides of the stage with Juillet going out one minute before Caitlyn. As Juillet was walking back to thunderous applause, Caitlyn stepped out on the stage, heading to the runway. When Juillet was three-quarters of the way back, Caitlyn was about to pass her. Suddenly Caitlyn lost her footing and stumbled into Juillet, causing Juillet to go tumbling off the runway. She fell five feet down, landing head first in a row of camera equipment and stage apparatus. The audience screamed. People rushed to Juillet. She was unconscious, and it appeared she was seriously injured with not only a severe head injury, but possibly a broken neck.

Caitlyn scrambled up from the runway floor and peered down, feigning concern and screaming out, "Oh my God, someone call an ambulance." Carla and Anja came running out and saw Caitlyn with tears in her eyes, holding onto one shoe in her hand and limping. "Cait, are you alright?" Then they looked over the edge of the runway and saw a horrifying scene.

No one could be sure, but from all appearances, it did look like an unfortunate freak accident. Juillet would never model again.

"Okay, I'll try to call them back," she said over her shoulder. "I hope these don't take up my whole afternoon," she said, grumbling, slamming the door behind her.

There it was. A message from a Dr. Christiansen. She was not sure what the hell that was about. Probably wanting a formal gown for his trophy wife for some dreary event. The name seemed familiar, but since she did not pay attention to world affairs, it really did not ring a bell.

"Guess I'll get this one over with. Don't know why he is calling me instead of letting Christine handle it as is the normal protocol," she said as she continued to complain. Being a big-shot doctor, I guess he thinks he deserves to go to the top with his request. What a joke, seeing as I'm really just a figurehead here, she thought, laughing to herself. Oh well, who am I to spoil the facade? But then I am the Caitlyn Sarantino of Caitlyn Couture. Shaking her head, she picked up the phone and dialed.

CHAPTER 9

Johann looked up from his medical journal when his cell phone blared an oldie song from the twenty-twenties. He quickly grabbed it and looked at the ID. It read Caitlyn Couture. It's now or never. A hint of doubt crept over him, but there was no turning back.

"Dr. Christianson," he answered, trying to sound professional.

"Ah, yes, Dr. Christianson," responded Caitlyn, thinking surely this was some sixty-something-old dude. "How may I help you today?" laying on her sweetness as thick as she could while gritting her teeth. She was still stewing as she flipped through the latest fashion catalog while returning this call.

"I was wondering if it would be possible to confer with you regarding a custom design dinner dress for my…" he suddenly could not remember what he had told Christine—his mother, grandmother or aunt, "Ahhh," he stammered.

"Your mother, I believe you had said, according to the message I got." She raised her eyebrows and shook her head in disbelief at this idiot as she continued to flip pages, hoping this call would be finished soon.

"Ah, yeah, that's right, my mother." It was going even worse than he had envisioned. Crap, I sound like an imbecile, he thought to himself.

Now Caitlyn was suspicious, as he sounded so much younger than she had imagined. Wonderful, a stalker or paparazzi. But he did sound intriguing.

"Maybe you can come by tomorrow, say elevenish?" she said as she put down the catalog and thumbed through her schedule. Phew, she thought, nothing at eleven. I've got to meet this bozo, if for no other reason than to satisfy my curiosity.

"That will be fine," he responded. He grabbed a towel to wipe the sweat off his brow. "I look forward to seeing, ah, the fabrics and designs. This is a surprise for, ah, my mother. She never thinks she needs a new dress but we have a very special occasion coming up," he lied.

Something really sounded fishy to Caitlyn, especially forgetting who the dress was for and then saying it was for a special occasion without really saying what. But, whatever, she thought. Who cares, as long as he spends a bundle?

"Good then. I will see you tomorrow."

After they hung up, he was thinking how oddly similar her voice was to Peyton's. Maybe different accented words, but the voice was the same. This is going to be so weird. He sure wished he could take Kirt. He got up and went to his closet. I might as well pick my wardrobe. I have to be a sexy dude for her to even give me a second glance. He was getting nervous about trying to compete in her world. He suspected she had an unlimited supply of international playboys with millions of dollars just in pocket change.

He looked in the mirror by his closet door and groaned. His hair was so out of control. Kirt had started to call him a mop head. But he liked it. It was carefree and didn't conform to that of the typical medical doctor. Mad scientist, maybe. He picked out a stone-colored cashmere sweater, jeans and chocolate-brown, suede sport jacket. He added his favorite brown suede boots to the look. He strode back out to the kitchen and sat down at the counter, wondering if this whole thing was crazy.

Kirt came sauntering in, kicking the front door shut with his foot, backwards, as he was loaded down with grocery bags in both hands. "All right, my friend," he announced. "Tonight we will toast and feast for your probable last supper of sanity." He had two New York steaks, two imported bottles of French wine, a huge long fresh, out-of-the-oven loaf of French bread and two six-inch long potatoes. Kirt loved to cook, but tonight was going to be easy compared to his complicated, exquisite German Wiener-schnitzel or meatball extraordinaire.

Johann laughed and slapped him on his back, almost dislodging the precious cargo. He grabbed one bag and they marched into the kitchen.

"Joey, what's the scoop? When is the rendezvous?" he asked, curiosity killing him.

"Tomorrow, around 11:00 a.m.," as he popped the cork on the wine.

"Wow," Kirt said as he grabbed a wine glass, stretching his arm in Johann's direction.

As Johann poured, he said, "I hope I know what I'm doing, Kirt. I've already screwed up my tale about who I was getting the dress for. I can't keep my facts, er, my lies straight. You know I'm a terrible liar."

"Hey, once she sees you, it won't matter, bro. She is going to fall madly in love with you," he said with a laugh.

"Don't know about that. She's used to the best-looking and well-built dudes in the universe. Why would I be a turn-on?"

"Well, you are a doctor. Don't all girls still want to marry a doctor? Besides, you are a famous, world-renown, doctor."

"Well, she sure didn't seem to know who I am. I don't think she impresses easily anyway. Gee, reminds me of Peyton, sort of. Besides, she does haute couture for royalty, world-famous types and rich folks. I certainly do not fit any of those categories."

"Joey, lets face it. You're a regular guy. Maybe that's just what she needs now. Besides, I wouldn't exactly call you poor. You're a millionaire in your own right. Just not a billionaire," he laughed. "And you do work hard for your reward."

"That's true," he admitted. "Alright, enough of the pep talk. Just wish you could go with me without it looking like you were my boyfriend," he shrugged.

Kirt grilled the steak and soon they were enjoying the feast, drinking wine and laughing raucously.

It was 5:30 a.m. and as usual, Johann was awake and ready to head out the door for his morning ritual. It was getting progressively chillier in the mornings, so he threw on his fleece running suit. He spent the next hour contemplating the day ahead as he jogged around Central Park.

By 10:45 he was dressed, coiffed, blown-dry as best he could and smelling great. He never used cologne, preferring to exude a hint of fresh soap from his shower. He called down to his friend and driver, Andre.

Kirt had already put in three hours of work via his computer. He came out of his office and whistled. "Hey man, you look great. Text me when you can, like when she isn't looking," he begged.

"Kirt, like I'm going to send you blow-by-blow action—forget it. You will just have to wait until I'm on my way home." With that, he waved and disappeared out the door. It was only a fifteen-minute drive to her fashion house. The traffic was light for a change.

The car pulled up and a waiting bellman was immediately at his door. "Good morning, sir," he greeted Johann.

"Good morning to you." Johann then poked his head back into the car. "I'm not sure how long I will be, Andre. I will call you as soon as I know." He thought to himself, this could be over in a matter of minutes. He never was one to exude confidence. But then he never cared about impressing people either. He was kind of like a take it or leave it sort of guy. He only cared about being the man his parents would be proud of, certainly not about being a superhero. He took a deep breath and pushed on with his ridiculous pursuit.

As he went through the door, a beautiful world of glamour appeared before him. He felt hugely out of place and somewhat self-conscious. He surmised that not many men frequented this place. But just as he thought that, out walked a very sharply dressed businessman who was waving good-bye to a very stunningly dressed forty-something lady. She turned to Johann and inquired, "Are you here to see Caitlyn?"

She was good, he thought, or my first guess was correct—not many men frequented this establishment. He nodded in agreement and was ushered into an opulent waiting room. There were beautiful soft, suede-covered, comfy chairs and couches as well as a large conference table of polished rosewood. There were floor-to-ceiling, handcrafted oak bookshelves loaded with catalogs and fabric books of all kinds. Mirrors, wall-mounted and freestanding, enhanced the room. There also was a design desk with a slanted top and high swivel chair presumably for designing creations on the spot. Pictures of familiar stars and dignitaries wearing the Caitlyn Couture line adorned the walls along with pictures and drawings of gowns and signature designs.

"Another world, indeed," he mumbled to himself. Certainly out of my league. I prefer my jeans and sweatshirts, he continued under his breath. But he must not have looked too bad as he saw eyes follow him as he was ushered into this room.

Christine then said, "Let me get you something. Would you care for a glass of Chardonnay or perhaps some Rhine wine?"

"Rhine sounds good," he smiled. Hopefully that would help dispel his nervousness.

As she handed him the glass of wine, Caitlyn waltzed in. "Dr. Christiansen, I presume," she snickered.

"That's me." The 'Dr. Livingston' reference did not elude him. He grinned at her with a knowing sparkle in his eyes.

When she took another look at him, all her suspicion melted away. His dark, saucy hair was in deep contrast to those penetrating sexy eyes. He had a Latin look, but the last name did not fit.

He was looking her over too. The comparison to Peyton was uncanny. Except for her absolutely gorgeous, blond hair, which most certainly was out of a bottle, her features were Peyton's. The dark, demure eyes, the long lashes, and a beautiful small nose with high cheekbones were identical. He could hardly take his eyes off of her. Then realizing he was staring, he looked away.

She was struck by him too. She was staring at his firm, toned body in his form-fitting jeans, wishing she could see his cute butt, but the expertly tailored sport jacket was covering it up. "You wanted to see me specifically about designing a gown for your mother?" she asked.

"Well, not exactly a gown," he said as he was clicking off dollar signs in his mind, knowing that would be far and above his financial means. "Just a dinner outfit." Even his vernacular sounded like a real amateur.

Caitlyn laughed. "Not your thing, is it Dr. Christiansen?"

"Please, call me Johann," he insisted.

"Okay, Johann. Let me show you some off-the- rack designs that you could order in her dress size."

"Sounds perfect." Thankful for her insight, he breathed a sigh of relief.

She buzzed Christine, who came into the room almost instantly. "Please bring the latest of our dinner collection for Dr. Christiansen's perusal."

"Sure thing." Within minutes she returned with fifteen dresses, all exquisite.

Observing his awkwardness, she asked just a few select questions about his mother, then selected four for him to choose from. He picked a beautiful dress in a light coral of plush, Italian baby camel hair, the softest and finest in the world. His mother was not one to go for plunging necklines, and this neckline was high but attractive.

Caitlyn's choices were right on. Very aware that even this successful doctor probably did not have the means to afford her clothing line, Caitlyn almost gave the dress away.

"It is five hundred dollars," she lied. Christine smiled, but kept her composure.

"Sounds perfect," he said, giving a smile of relief. "That's a deal." And they shook hands. "Since we successfully accomplished this task," Johann said, "why don't I take you to lunch to celebrate?" Being so presumptuous that this world-renown designer would even consider such a thing, Johann just went for it.

"Since it really was a task for you, I think lunch is in order," she agreed. "Just let me get my coat."

Johann was almost beside himself. She was gorgeous, intelligent and a hugely successful businesswoman. And known all over the world. What more could he want?

CHAPTER 10

After an extraordinary gourmet lunch at the most prestigious restaurant in New York, Johann dropped Caitlyn back at her design studio. It was after 4:00 pm, and the last few hours had been indescribable She was chatty, funny and seemed to really enjoy his company. Now armed with numbers for both her home and cell phones, he figured he must have scored pretty high on her list.

As he arrived home, he barely got in the door when he heard, "Why didn't you text me, you clod? I have been pacing for hours," Kirt shouted.

"Kirt, I never had a moment away from her except for a brief trip to the men's room. Really can't text and pee at the same time."

"Well, you could have voice texted me," he bellowed. Johann just rolled his eyes. "So?" pleaded Kirt. "Tell me," he insisted.

"Kirt, she is unbelievable. I felt totally comfortable with her too. I think this relationship is going to work for me. My heart has been racing out of my chest. She even gave me her numbers to call for our next date. Can you believe it? She wants to see me again." He was like a schoolboy. "Thank you so much for suggesting I look for her."

"Well, I hope I did not make a mistake in giving you that advice, my friend. Do you plan to investigate her?"

"I suppose that would be the smart thing to do. You can do it, buddy, but I don't think you're going to find anything perverse about this magnificent woman," he remarked, so sure of this remarkable find.

"Listen, Joey, I will give you just three more days to come down off your cloud and get back to some serious work." Kirt was feeling the pressure of impending issues that needed Johann's attention.

"Okay, slave driver. But for three more days I am going to wine and dine her and maybe a few other things," he responded with a glint in his eye.

"Yeah, you do that bud." Kirt had hoped Caitlyn would be the girl of his dreams and not the biggest mistake of his life. Unfortunately, she had a reputation that Johann did not know about. Yet! Kirt and his CIA buddies already had been digging up dirt that had him really concerned. But she was young, and maybe her careless, promiscuous days were behind her, and she would straighten up her act and grow into a respectable entrepreneur.

Johann was now working days and spending evenings getting to know Caitlyn. It had been several weeks and he was becoming more and more captivated by her.

They had just finished a pizza and were now sprawled out on the thick, soft carpet in her immense, casual living room. A warm fire was glowing, adding a romantic ambiance to the room. Caitlyn was on her fourth glass of wine. She did not appear intoxicated, just relaxed and chatty.

"You're a better imbiber than I, Caitlyn. I can barely have two glasses without feeling tipsy."

"I've had a lot more practice," she quipped with a quick little laugh. "In fact, I'm tired of wine," as she got up and walked over to a well-stocked wet bar. She pulled out an aged brandy and poured it into two brandy snifters.

"Geez, Caitlyn," he complained. "I do have to work tomorrow and my taskmaster is going to be pretty pissed if I awake with a humongous hangover."

She cozied up to him and stared into his searing blue eyes. She ran her finger down his face to the unique cleft in his chin. God she was irresistible, thought Johann. He grabbed the glass and downed the brandy. He set the glass down and drew Caitlyn to him. He took her face in his hands and gently kissed her voluptuous lips. Next he kissed her neck and suddenly hot desire swept over him.

Caitlyn was now undressing him in a frenzy and it was not long before they were both naked in front of the flickering fire. They spent the rest of the evening making love and exploring each other's body.

It was getting late, almost midnight, when Johann said, "Caitlyn, I don't know how I can bear to leave you, but I must go home as I have an unbelievably difficult day tomorrow. I have to go to the UN to attend a very pertinent conference. I still have to polish my speech."

"Oh, Johann," she whined, "tell Kirt to do it and stay here with me."

"Too funny, Caitlyn. I must go." He dressed in a flash and headed to the door. Caitlyn pouted, quite obviously she was used to having her own way.

"I'll call you between meetings, Cait. You know I will be over tomorrow night, but rather late. Our conference includes a dinner meeting."

"That's not fair. They get to have you all day and evening and I get you only for a few hours," Caitlyn protested. She was still pouting her voluptuous lips and begging with her large, sumptuous, chocolate eyes.

"Yes, but the hours you have me are much more fun and meaningful," responded Johann, trying hard to placate her.

She continued to pressure him. "Well, I get you for the upcoming weekend. I am not sharing you one iota. There is a grand opening Friday night at the art museum as well as the introduction of an up-and-coming new artist. We must go," she insisted.

"Cait, I will have to check my schedule. You have to understand that I don't work a nine-to-five job. I am more of a sixteen hour, seven days a week, work when necessary kind of guy."

"Well, we're just going to have to change that," she insisted. Her demeanor changed radically from that coy little nymph to a determined woman who did not take "no" for an answer. The change was lost on Johann.

He looked at her sultry eyes and very inviting body. "I will try to change things around this weekend, Caitlyn," as he caved in to her.

She grinned and slid her hand across his chest and down his abdomen. Johann grabbed her and brought her into a tight embrace and kissed her. These weeks had been very intense and he felt overpowered by Caitlyn and had been finding it very difficult to pull away from her to leave every night. He finally released her and looked into her eyes. "Caitlyn, you are so incredibly beautiful. I don't know how much longer I can continue to leave you at night to trudge back to my home."

"You know, Johann, you can just stay with me full-time. I have never been with anyone as gentle and loving as you. I am falling hopelessly in love with you."

"I wish I could. But I have enormous responsibility right now that truly needs my attention." He pulled on his jacket and gave her one last long kiss. He was starting to weaken. "I'll talk with Kirt and see if I could skip out a little early for your event Friday night."

"I think Mr. Kirt will need to be told what the priorities in your life are now. After all, my love, you have to have a life of your own."

Johann suddenly felt a little uneasy about Caitlyn's demands. "Well, it's not quite as easy as that." He felt a fleeting chill. He brushed it off, doubting his own emotion.

Sensing his pulling away, she cleverly started to caress his neck and moved her body into his.

"Aw, come on, Caitlyn. I really have to go." She had powerful control over his now weakening resistance. Within minutes, he again found himself naked in her irresistible embrace, taking her with more fire than before. She could turn him into a madman with raging desire and with no ability to stop until he exploded within her. She screamed with complete satisfaction as he brought her to ecstasy over and over again.

They both lay there in front of the fiercely flickering fire, shuddering from the amazing sex they had just enjoyed. "Caitlyn, you are the most amazing woman I have ever been with."

"Johann, you are the one who is incredible," she countered breathlessly. "We are so good together. I will never let you go, so don't even try," she warned.

He laughed. "You don't have to worry about that."

"Let's get married," she said suddenly. "Right away, just do it." She rolled onto him, skin to skin, caressing his chest.

Johann was totally stunned. He looked at her with puppy-dog eyes. "Caitlyn, I think we need to slow down just a bit. That takes a lot of planning and ..." She cut him off.

"No," she interrupted. "No planning. That's what's so exciting about it."

"We've been together only four weeks. I know it has been amazing, but we have to really be sure this is what we both want. And for the long haul."

"Then how about five weeks from now. Is that enough planning time for you?" she asked pleadingly.

"Let me get back to you," he chuckled and kissed her on her cute forehead. "You're a trip, Miss Caitlyn Sarantino. You are wearing me down. I'm a confirmed bachelor, you know."

"Not for long," she countered. She was snuggling into a fluffy robe, but slowly so he could again get a good look at what he could have. Forever.

He quickly redressed, and this time kept his distance from her and flew out the door. His car was waiting and he told Andre, "Get me home fast before I change my mind."

Caitlyn was totally in love with Johann, at least in her version of love. She had to find a way to make him marry her so she would have him to herself. She would see to it he'd give up this crazy work schedule and instead spend his days and nights with her, traveling the world. No more one night stands or weeklong orgies with some Italian lover--well, at least not indiscreet liaisons. Johann did please her exceptionally well sexually. He turned her on constantly and she could seduce him anytime and anywhere she wanted. Perfect! She had her perfect boy toy. She would make sure his lifework became her instead of that boring scientific research and those silly clone people. He had more important things to do, like please her.

She was already missing him, wanting to have sex again. Once she got turned on, it was hard to turn off. She called down to security.

"Mr. Max, could you stop up for a second? I need something fixed." Within minutes Max was at the door.

"Howdy, Ms. Sarantino. What do you need fixed?" He grinned, playing coy, looking down at his feet.

"You know, cowboy," as she pulled him in.

Within seconds she was ripping at his clothes. He swept her into his arms and carried her to her bed. He was in her, pounding her, prompting squeals of delight. She was one hot lady, and he pleased her over and over. She just could never get enough, he was thinking. He often came on request even after her one-night stands. Maybe they just warmed her up for him. But he didn't care. He got his booty call constantly and was more than happy to please.

She finally gave one last gasp, and he finished his obligatory orgasm with a shout of his own. He collapsed next to her.

"Am I done here, madam?"

She laughed, "Yeah, get out of here, you sex slave."

She finally was satisfied enough to fall asleep.

He let himself out the door and locked it behind him. I love this shift, he grinned to himself.

Johann grudgingly got up when his alarm went off at 5:30 am. But instead of his usual run, he nursed a headache and slight nausea. He downed some aspirin and sat at the table drinking a cup of strong coffee.

Man, I hope I can shake this before Kirt drifts in. I've got one hour, he lamented to himself. He was not a drinker and always paid for it the next day. Why did he allow Caitlyn to ply him with that rotgut. He smiled though as he remembered the wonderful night of passionate lovemaking. He was falling for her. He couldn't help it. She had a strange hold on him. He was intoxicated with her.

Yikes, wait till Kirt hears about the marriage proposal. He's going to flip out. He was laughing out loud.

"What's so funny?" Johann heard from the kitchen doorway. Kirt barely had his eyes open and was up earlier than usual.

"You look terrible," Johann said as he gave Kirt a cursory glance.

"Talk about me? Look at you. You look green. Are you okay?" he quipped back.

"Sure, uh, just a little tired," he lied.

"Ahhh, looks more like hung over," he countered, as he leaned down and got a closer look at Johann's red eyes.

"Yeah, well, I did have a little more than I'm used to," he admitted. "But I'll be fine in a few hours, I hope."

"You know you are a lousy drinker, bro. You have to convince Caitlyn to go easy on you. You are not one of her playboys."

"Ahhh, Caitlyn. She is quite the seductress. Kirt, I have never had anyone like her, ever. She takes me places I could never ever have imagined. I cannot even imagine porn turning me on the way she can."

"Right, Joey. Oh boy, she sounds dangerous," he said it chidingly and he actually really meant it.

"She wants me, Kirt. I mean really wants me. She wants me to marry her. Like now or in five weeks."

"Are you nuts?" shouted Kirt. The coffee he had just brought up to his lips now spilled down across his chest as he whirled around to face Johann.

"Well, I didn't say I'd do it-exactly." He looked up at Kirt with a sheepish look on his face.

"What EXACTLY did you say?" Kirt's face was turning red.

"I told her I had to consider it." Johann diverted his eyes to his coffee cup, afraid to meet Kirt's.

"Consider it, Johann, please. You must slow down. You don't even know her," he pleaded. "Sure she's great in the sack, but you need to get to know her."

"So far, Kirt, she's extraordinary. But there is one little thing I see coming out in her."

"Oh, yeah? What would that be?" Kirt questioned, his impatience, definitely escalating.

"She's a little spoiled. She kind of wants things her way. Even wants to change my schedule to fit hers."

At that, Kirt exploded. "You got to be kidding. Ahh, RED FLAG, Joey."

"Ya think?" Johann asked. His head still throbbed and he wished he had never started this conversation.

"Sounds like a control freak maybe? Take another week and really explore her head, buddy. I know you won't stay out of her pants, but please don't let that sway your judgment."

Kirt knew he could not tell him the truth about what he had found. He had to let Johann find out for himself and make his own decision about her.

"Hit the shower," Kirt commanded. Johann slowly rose, holding his head and stomach, grimacing in unrelieved pain.

CHAPTER 11

Caitlyn, dressing for the museum opening, expected Johann any minute. She was ecstatic that she was able to persuade Johann to slip out early from his awful meetings to escort her to this very prestigious event. She could not wait to show him off. She knew everyone would be mad with jealousy over her ability to snag this very important hunk.

She slipped on her gown, a one-shouldered, floor-length silk of an exquisite shade of lavender. She had gotten the material from Ceylon, and the dress was custom made for her by Christine.

That Christine, she was thinking, she not only runs my couture superbly, but designs and makes a perfect gown for me and on a moment's notice. I really should give her a raise. Most likely, Caitlyn's scattered, drug-damage brain would forget that thought by morning. Her makeup artist/hairdresser, Judah, had finished doing her magic, so she was ready to roll, looking like a flawless celebrity

She walked over to the bar and unlocked a drawer. Inside was an array of designer drugs from opiates to sedatives. She brought out a small amount of cocaine and sniffed it. The pleasure it produced was awesome and immediate. She grabbed some tablets of other designer drugs and placed them in a small gold pouch to put in her purse. She wanted to continue to have pleasurable feelings and knew the wine or alcohol that would be flowing just wouldn't do it for her. Her tolerance had grown tremendously over the years, so combining all of it was tolerated very well. So she thought.

She noticed, though, that lately it was getting harder and harder to get up in the morning. The constant cough was bugging her too. She managed to suppress it for the most part with cough suppressants of codeine. She did not have a lot of energy either, but attributed that to her constant, busy life. She hated looking at herself without makeup too. Her skin looked dower. But with makeup on, she looked like dynamite. And around Johann, she was able to hide all these depressing things.

She finished dressing and gave a last minute spritz to her hair. She smelled luscious and looked gorgeous. Judah had added more long luminous eyelashes to her already spectacular ones to give her eyes an even more alluring look. Her eye shadow was a smoky gray and the black liner brought out the large, almond shape of her eyes, enhancing her chocolate-brown irises. She skillfully added more rosy color to her cheeks and a bright rose lipstick to her voluptuous lips. She knew instinctively that she looked irresistible.

Just then the doorbell rang. She blotted her lips then glided to the door, feeling extremely mellow. She felt excited to see her new love, but also was feeling the effects of the long-lasting cocaine. As she yanked open the door, she flung herself into Johann's outstretched arms. He was blown away with her beauty. "Caitlyn, you are incredible." He pulled her closer and kissed her passionately, wanting more than the kiss.

Caitlyn finally pulled away and stood there at arm's length. "Johann, you're just going to have to wait." Yet she teased him by rubbing up against him and caressing his thighs. "Geez, Cait. If you want me to wait, you're going to have to stop that."

"Okay, but just keep that thought. We we'll back here in no time," she promised.

"Yeah, like what, five hours?" he protested.

"You'll live," she teased. "Maybe we could find a secluded spot at the museum," she added.

"Hmmm, that's a thought."

With that, he helped her on with her floor-length matching coat and whisked her out the door to his waiting car.

CHAPTER 12

"So, Barron, when do you go in?" Abby asked. Barron and Claire were helping their two six-year-old twins finish their homework. The new adorable baby girl Paige swung in her infant swing, watching all of the action around her. She was trying hard to stay awake, but her eyelids kept closing. She finally gave up and fell asleep.

"I'm scheduled Wednesday morning. The surgery should take about four hours, barring any complications. I will be on the heart/lung machine probably for three to four days. Maybe I will be a fast regenerator and grow my new heart in two days," he said with a laugh.

His original human had suffered a heart attack. Over time he had occluded most of his coronary arteries. In his early forties, he already needed to have his heart replaced. Barron was excited to be donating this vital organ. After all, that was the reason for his existence. "It's too bad human beings can't regenerate whole organs like we can. They can grow skin and some nerve cells, but it takes forever. Just glad we can do it three times," he grinned, "or it would be curtains for me." He ran his fingers across his throat like he was cutting it with a knife.

Claire glared at him. "Barron, don't scare the kids," she warned. Actually, the twins were giggling.

Abby said, "I hope everything goes really well, Barron and you come home safe and sound. We'll miss you. But we will come see you at the hospital; you know we will." Abby and Peyton were at the table with the twins going over an agenda for an upcoming community board meeting, white wine in hand.

"Yuck," Peyton spoke up, a big frown on her face. "I hate hospitals. I get dizzy and clammy just seeing all those IVs in people and all that other hospital stuff. I'll go, but you will have to lead me, Abby, as I am going to have my eyes shut." She shuttered and crossed her arms in front of her in a tight hug at the thought of walking down a hospital corridor.

"You are such a wimp, Peyton. I'm thankful you didn't pick nursing for your college major."

"Ah, yeah, Abby. Like I could deal with puking and peeing patients. If I had to choose, I would rather work with dead people. At least they don't do those things. How would I be as the community mortician? Course the work would be slow with our negligible death rate."

Abby burst out laughing at the thought. The kids really giggled now. Claire and Barron were busily putting together a simple, delicious, vegetable casserole to go in the oven.

Claire asked. "So what about those human specimens you saw weeks ago? I haven't even had a chance to ask you. Were they what you expected?"

"No, not at all," said Peyton, avoiding direct eye contact. "I really didn't know what to expect. The experience was really, ahhh, different." She was drumming her fingernails on the counter. Just thinking about the visit brought back fond memories. Taking another swallow of wine, she looked at Abby.

"I know what you mean, Peyton. That Miguel Tavares kept staring at me. Really strange, but I actually felt attracted to him. It was really, really weird," admitted Abby, blushing slightly.

"Hmmm, Abby, my dear sister, you never told me that. We need to talk," Peyton said as she tilted her head and squinted her eyes.

Barron and Claire laughed at the two of them. "You two are up to something, as usual," said Claire. "I knew the day you both arrived together twenty-eight years ago that we were going to have our hands full. Neither of you has disappointed us either. Two mischievous peas in a pod," she said grinning and beaming with pride.

Peyton and Abby laughed and gave each other a hug and kiss. "Thank goodness we were born the same day and ironically at the same hospital, arriving here to the loving arms of you guys," Abby said with tears in her eyes.

Peyton added, "We may have been a handful, Claire, but we sure loved our childhood together, thanks to you and Barron." Peyton suddenly took a really long look at Abby. She noted that she, like her, did not look twenty years old anymore. She really had not paid attention to their looks until lately. She first questioned her own changing face and now Abby's.

"Why are you staring at me, Peyton?" asked Abby. " Just because I don't have makeup on, you don't have to stare." She was laughing now. "Do I have a zit or something?"

Peyton shook her head and said, "It's nothing, Abs. I was just looking at your beautiful, flawless skin." It was indeed beautiful and flawless, but had a hint of, of all things, wrinkles at the outside aspect of her eyes; just slight and mostly when she smiled or laughed. Very unusual for a twenty-year-old, she thought. Neither Claire nor Barron showed any lines in their faces. But she had noticed just a trace on her own face, just a hint, not even enough for anyone else to notice, she hoped. When Abby confessed, even jokingly, about a possible attraction to Miguel, it hit home with her as she also had very strange feelings when Johann looked her. His touch induced electrical shocks throughout her body. She could not explain it. She even searched Internet sites for any clone abnormality that might explain it. She found nothing relating to this. It didn't happen. These, she had determined, were like human emotions, something clones were supposedly devoid of.

So why her and why Abby? And what does this mean for them?

CHAPTER 13

The elaborate dinner of filet mignon and scallops was well worth skipping Kirt's boring dinner with diplomats. But now Johann squirmed in his seat, obligated to listen to the speakers drone on. He squeezed Caitlyn's hand. She immediately pulled her hand away, which he found disconcerting, but he shrugged it off. Johann was still captivated by Caitlyn and amazed at all the people who constantly surrounded her. The museum venue transformed a massive hallway into an elegant, intimate dining area. It had soft lights and glowing candles at each table. The power people were in abundance, and it was obvious that this was a very significant money-raiser for the art museum. This event relied heavily on huge donations and endowments to maintain, attract and obtain collections from all over the world.

Caitlyn seemed to be getting restless. He gave her a wink like he understood. These things could drag on way longer than he liked. He then noticed a slight tremor in her hands as she lifted her wine glass. "Cait, are you okay?" Johann inquired, a little concerned at this point.

"I'm fine," she lied. "Just a slight headache coming on. No big deal." Damn, she thought, I need a fix. "Please hand me my purse and I'll see if I have any aspirin."

As Johann reached for the bag from the back of her chair, it slipped to the floor. Some of the contents spilled out, including a gold pouch. Its latch had opened and pills spilled on the floor. He quickly kneeled down to scoop them up. I guess the five-second rule will apply here, he thought, knowing he could scoop them up in a couple seconds. He would not tell Caitlyn her Tylenol or aspirins had hit the dirty floor. Caitlyn was unaware the pouch had opened so was not at all concerned. As Johann was about to put the pills back in the pouch, he took a second look. Curiously, they were not aspirin or Tylenol as he had expected. There were uppers and downers and solid cocaine. There also was a cylinder, which he suspected was for a pulverized drug. He put the pouch back into the purse. He felt the blood drain from his head, shock setting in. Being disturbed was putting it mildly. He handed her the purse, still reeling from what he had witnessed. He was trying to process it.

Caitlyn excused herself from the table to go to the ladies' room to "fix her makeup" as she put it. Johann, still in disbelief, started to sweat. He felt pain in the pit of his stomach. His mind was swirling with the thought of his beloved Caitlyn being a drug addict. This would ruin everything. Tears were welling up in his eyes. He had to know.

Caitlyn returned to the table, a little wobbly, but back to her gregarious, chatty self. He surveyed her closely. Her tremor was gone. That clinched it. His suspicions were true. He was now exploding inside.

"Johann, dear," she started. "There is a premier in Paris next week, and I have booked our flight for Wednesday. I will show you all the sights of that fabulous city. It's my second home. My mother lives there more than she lives here. We'll make it a short visit-like just two weeks. We will have …"

"Caitlyn," protested Johann, cutting her off in mid-sentence. "I can't go to Paris now and be gone two weeks. I am in the middle of a critical mission and will be traveling to multiple countries with President Tavares and Kirt. How on earth could you ever expect me to drop my work and gallivant to Paris?" He was really on edge now.

Caitlyn stared at him, taken aback with this sudden negative outburst. She put on that now familiar pout. "Of course you can, Johann." She moved her hand to his thigh under the table.

"Caitlyn, that's not going to work!" He was suddenly aware that maybe Caitlyn wasn't as he wanted her to be, the perfect love of his life. He was starting to see things that scared him to death. Caitlyn seemed to ignore his obvious change in attitude.

"Johann, my love, what better place is there to get married? We don't need a horde of people, just a small private ceremony at our family country villa."

Things were starting to escalate. She was becoming more and more demanding and just not getting it. Is this a drug effect, the real

Caitlyn, or both?

"Honey," she continued, "you will call Kirt and tell him you will be out of circulation until next month. I'm sure he can handle that detail, right? After all, that's his job, right?" She said that with a sneer, alluding to her perception that Kirt merely was a well-paid employee, like her staff.

"Actually Caitlyn, Kirt is my best friend and he is also my business partner. More important, he is the best manager that I could ever ask for. He stays on top of all the business details that continue to surround me. But that said, he is more like my brother."

Caitlyn was tearing up now, changing tactics.

"Caitlyn, save it. I'm not going."

Now she was getting furious.

"Cait, this really is not the place to discuss this. People are starting to stare. Let's go," he demanded. He got up, pulled her chair out.

She grabbed her purse and rose in a huff. "Fine," she said, clearly becoming more and more unraveled.

As they walked out, the light caught her dark eyes in such a way that Johann noticed a faint yellowing of her sclera, the white part of her eyes. How had he not noticed that before? It hit him that there was something very serious going on with her liver. She gave out a cough as she walked hurriedly beside him. Her cough was now becoming evident as her cough medication wore off. His mind was whirling. It all was coming together: Serious drugs in her purse, heavy alcohol consumption and who knows what else. Was she also promiscuous without regard for protecting against STDs? Luckily he used protection, even when their lovemaking was spontaneous. He never let himself be stupid, even in the event of sudden passion. He was now more than convinced that his dream was totally smashed. He knew what he needed to do- get out of this relationship immediately.

Oh my God. He suddenly had a gut-wrenching realization. She was going to need a transplant of her liver and maybe her heart as well, from what he could observe without physically assessing her. Peyton, oh my God, he screamed to himself. He knew what was coming and suddenly thought he was going to vomit.

Caitlyn looked at him. "Good Lord, Johann. You look like you've seen a ghost. Let's just talk about this reasonably. I'm sure when we get back to my place, you will have come to your senses." She was counting on it. She knew her talent of seduction would work as usual. He couldn't resist her.

Johann called Andre who arrived within minutes. He dialed in Caitlyn's address and the car took off through the streets of New York. They arrived within fifteen minutes after a ride in total silence.

"Andre," Johann said, "please see Miss Sarantino to her door for me. I have a splitting headache."

Caitlyn stared at him in disbelief. Andre opened her door and gestured for her to get out, offering his arm.

"Johann," she pleaded.

"No, Caitlyn. I really am feeling sick and just want to get home. I will call you."

She got out, refusing Andre's assistance. The doorman opened the door, "Good evening, Miss Sarantino." She pushed past him without a word.

Andre shrugged and said, "Women." The doorman just laughed. "She's her typical self."

It was 10:00 pm when Johann arrived home. Kirt was still up working as usual on his computer. "Hey, Joey, que pasa?" as he looked up to see a very disturbed Johann. "Seriously, bud, what's up?"

"Kirt, I don't know where to begin. I guess I should have done my homework instead of relying on my libido."

Kirt knew what was coming. He had really hoped all his research would have been proven wrong, but apparently not.

"Kirt, this girl is in trouble. Her apparent out-of-control life has her now in medical crisis. Her liver is shot. She has jaundice and has developed a cough, which I suspect may be related to heart disease. She may have developed a cardiomegaly or left ventricular hypertrophy or…"

"Johann," Kirt interrupted, "English please."

"Sorry. It appears she has obstruction in her liver and her heart muscle may be failing, causing her lungs to build up fluid, hence the cough. Her lifestyle, it seems, has been atrocious and has contributed to her failing organs. How it took me so long to see the truth about Caitlyn baffles me. Kirt, how could I have been so blind? I almost made the biggest mistake of my life."

"But you didn't, bro. Your good judgment finally prevailed. You were just swept off your feet, and your brain took a leave of absence."

"Kirt, we've got to go to Community 27 immediately."

"Are you serious? What is that going to accomplish, Doctor? You know there is no chance of you and Peyton pairing up."

"I know that, but I have to warn her."

"What are you talking about, Joey? If her parts are needed, that's what she's here for. She is Caitlyn's clone. Caitlyn is, by law, entitled to her."

"No, I can't, I just can't stand the thought of that," screamed Johann as he paced back and forth.

"We'll talk about it tomorrow," Kirt said, anxious to end this discussion and get to bed.

"Okay, but tomorrow we are traveling to Community 27."

"Alright, but we'll take my jet. I'm not up for a four-hour-vehicle ride to and from," Kirt pronounced.

"Sounds perfect. Is Miguel still in New York? Maybe he would like to tag along."

"I'll text him right now in case he is still up." Kirt got an immediate response-YES, YES, YES.

"Okay, So Miguel will fly over with us," said Kirt.

"Sounds like a plan, right?" Johann asked with a deep sigh.

"Okay, then. Shower and bed. Now!" shouted Kirt.

Johann was totally exhausted from his trying day and emotional distress that ensued. He conked out the minute his head hit the pillow.

For Kirt, it took a little longer. He was worried about what tomorrow would bring. It probably was going to be worse than he could ever envision.

CHAPTER 14

Thankfully, air traffic at Teteboro was slow. Within minutes of arriving at the airport, pre-checks were done and they were next in line for takeoff. Johann, staring out at the runway, started to rant.

"Miguel, it was a nightmare. I can't fathom how it took me so long to realize Caitlyn was a time bomb."

"Ay caramba Johann. It's happened to all of us at one time or another."

"She had me totally spellbound. What power she had over me. The sex with her was so addictive; I was unable to even think straight. I missed the destructive signs for so long until they hit me over the head." Johann looked crushed, now staring down at his feet.

"Put it behind you, bud. Let's get back to work. Good to have you back full-time, mind and body," said Miguel, extending his hand to Johann. "Bienvenido, mi amigo."

They were now wheels up, cruising at thirty thousand feet and heading to Binghamton, New York, within the clone community boundaries. It seemed like no time at all and the wheels were coming down, touchdown moments away.

"Miguel, we do have some projects pending," said Johann, "but I have other things I need to address," he confessed, a somber look on his face.

"Okay. I hope it includes conferring with that awesome Abby. I'm so glad you needed my expertise today," he said, chuckling.

"What are you thinking? They're clones, damn it. Can you hear the gossip world-wide, that you had the hots for a clone, Miguel?" Johann said, clamping his lip and turning his head away.

"Remember, mi amigo, no one will know. They are cloistered.

There is no news to the outside world."

"Oh, duh," Johann said, nodding. "But they don't have the emotion wired in their brain like we humans, so what kind of relationship could there possibly ever be?" Johann was so conflicted.

"I know that's true, but for some reason I felt a connection with Abby. Really strange, knowing the biology," Miguel professed. "So why are we really coming here today, Johann? You clearly are not yourself and I hate to say it, you look like hell."

"I'll cut to the chase, amigo. I want to do some tests on Peyton. I have this uneasy feeling about her."

"Of course you do, dude. You're attracted to her. I get it. And the OH did not work out as you wanted."

"Miguel, you don't understand. Caitlyn is very ill. She will be asking for clone parts. I'll be damned if I will let anyone touch that precious Peyton. I know the dalliance with Caitlyn was just a crazy, desperate alternative for my real attraction to Peyton. How could I ever have thought it could work?" he said, rhetorically.

"Forget it. You screwed up. Literally."

"I must warn her. I know what's coming down."

The jet now on the ground, pulled up to the covered tarmac. A black SUV waited for them. Andre and Kirt slid out of the cockpit, opened the door, and bounded down the steps. They unloaded the attaché cases, backpacks and small luggage, into the back of the SUV. Andre got behind the wheel, and punched in the destination data in preparation for the next leg of the trip.

Kirt had called the night before to give Abby and Peyton a heads-up to their impending visit and ETA. It was now 8:30 am and they would be pulling up to the education center in one hour.

Miguel put an arm around Johann as they prepared to get into the car. "We'll work everything out. We've got your back."

For the first time in hours, a slight smile emerged on Johann's face.

CHAPTER 15

It had been over six weeks since their initial meeting. The weather was definitely fall-crisp during the day, but downright cold at night. They were expecting flurries in the next few days. This was so typical of upstate New York's quirky weather.

The guys arrived at 9:30 am and walked into the education center, finding the girls at work in Peyton's office. They were here on the pretext that they had a project to do in the community. Peyton was stunning, as usual, in soft, black slacks with a gray turtleneck sweater. A gold metal belt graced her slender hips. She wore black, suede platform heels that gave illusion of being taller than she actually was. Abby wore a violet sweater-dress, just down to mid-thigh. She wore black tights and ankle-high, black boots. Her white-blond hair fell down around her shoulders in soft curls, and her eyes took on a violet shade of blue.

Abby and Peyton jumped up and greeted them all with warm hugs. Miguel, smiling broadly, bringing out his deep dimples, kissed them both on each cheek.

"We are so pleased to have you back," gushed Abby, trying to stay professional. "We have a workstation set up for you."

"But before you get started, let's have some coffee and treats and catch up on what you guys have been up to," said Peyton.

Kirt glanced at Johann, unable to suppress a wide smile

"Yeah, well, umph," Johann said, clearing his throat. "We've been studying the reports from our previous trip here." He did not dare look Peyton in the face.

Peyton stared at him, cocking her head.

Kirt added, "And doing some field research work."

Miguel added, "We had a very successful conference at the UN with several world leaders."

Johann glared at Kirt. "I have not been making the best use of time but now am back on track." Johann finally looked at Peyton. She was more beautiful than ever. The gray sweater emphasized her sumptuous eyes and glowing face.

She, in turn, was mesmerized by his searing blue eyes. She was becoming more comfortable with him and had no inhibition to say whatever came into her head. Even his important position did not deter her. "So, your fieldwork. What exactly did that involve?" She had gotten a huge suspicion from Kirt's smirk and Johann's slight blush that it was something he preferred not to talk about. Peyton loved to see people squirm, so she pressed on. "So?" she asked, as she waited for him to answer.

Johann took her hand in his and said, "Peyton, you don't want to know and you don't need to know," as he glared again at Kirt.

Peyton's eyes flashed to Abby and they both broke out laughing. She gave up, knowing he wasn't going to break.

London then waltzed in and greeted everyone. Her brilliant red hair was flowing around her face. She carried a platter piled high with delicious-looking pastries that were a very low fat version, high in fiber and actually super healthy.

"Yum," exclaimed Kirt. And he was not talking about the pastries.

London wore a long, wool tweed skirt with a brown/charcoal sweater. Her green eyes sparkled with joy on seeing Kirt. "Hey guys. About time you got back here. Not that we need any help from you. But you do provide us clones a good study in human species behavior." They all laughed at silly London.

Kirt, especially, from day one, had said he would be very happy to stay here forever. He hated New York City and missed the days of long ocean voyages and yachting competitions. He did not need to be entertained. Nature entertained him fully. But of course, having a raving, beautiful, funny fraulein like London in his life wouldn't hurt. How ironic that these three guys and these three girls could come together one time and have an instant attraction. And that they were clones, added to an unexplainable mystery. After the regrettable liaison with Caitlyn, Johann knew he already loved Peyton. It had been instantaneous from day one and now unstoppable.

The coffee was so superb, the guys were asking for refills. It was evident that Johann and Miguel weren't too eager to stop their socializing and actually get to work. One hour ran into two, and they were still yakking and telling stories.

Johann sat with his coffee cup in both hands, staring into space, his mind wandering from the ongoing conversation. Somehow he would have to talk about why they were here. It was not going to be easy, but was certainly necessary.

Peyton and Abby finally stood up and announced they both needed to return to their work and get some pressing issues resolved. "I'm really sorry to end this intriguing discussion, but I have to get back to a professor who I am sure is pacing by now," said Peyton. "Nothing too urgent, but I did promise him a resolution today. How about dinner tonight? Our treat," she added. She sure was hoping they would be able to take some time off this evening, especially since they had goofed off most of the day. She was still under the illusion that they were here to work.

Johann looked up with his steel-blue eyes, sending her into that now familiar dizzying desire. "Of course, tonight," he replied. "We look forward to it, right Miguel, Kirt?"

"You bet," shot back Miguel and Kirt in unison. "I've been hankering for a beef-less steak since we left here weeks ago," Kirt said facetiously.

London sidled over to him. "Believe it, big guy, once you've broken that carnivorous habit, you will never go back."

Abby was now giggling, gesturing toward Miguel, and said, "I'm not sure this Brazilian could ever be converted."

Miguel grinned at her and said, "Hmmm, maybe it just takes the right convincing and lots and lots of vegetarian meals to convert me. I will have to spend a tremendous amount of time being taught the principles of it too. I have to be thoroughly prepared."

Abby retorted back, "Well, I know how precious little time you have, running the world and all. I too, have enormous responsibility in the day-to-day operations of this community. So, amigo, you will have to attend night school for your lessons."

Everyone cracked up at this point. Abby laughed hard, bending over, covering her mouth, and jerking back up, back and forth. Her long flaxen hair flew every which way. Miguel could hardly resist grabbing her and running his fingers through her locks. She was a vision of pure perfection. He certainly could understand Johann's obsession with Peyton as he, himself, was becoming overtaken by this indescribable creature.

"Okay, girlfriend, let's get them out of here and we get a little work done, so we won't be bothered tonight with phone calls," Peyton said with a snicker. "London, take these human aristocrats to the workstation and stay with them in case they need help with our advanced technology," she said, sarcastically. "Or maybe they're just imposters."

"Imposters?" Johann questioned with feigned hurt. "You don't think we are very important people with high worldly positions in the human world?"

"Sure, sure," Peyton replied. "I'm sure the humans think you're very important."

"But you don't?" he continued to push her.

"Look, I am not about to insult the person who is responsible for our welfare. I'm not that dumb." She grinned back at him with her teasing eyes. She gave him a wink, then turned on her heels and was out the door, heading to the boardroom.

He sat there staring out the doorway as she disappeared out of sight. All he could think about was Peyton. Somehow he was going to have to get his mind on his mission. They needed this time to plan their strategy. How was he going to deliver this urgent information to the girls? How would Peyton react? Would she be mad at him for interfering with her prime purpose, a purpose they were born with, the most important event in their clone lives?

What he was about to learn would shake him to the core.

CHAPTER 16

After the girls left, Johann, Kirt and Miguel huddled together. Kirt, talking in low tones, filled in Miguel on Johann's plight. They did not want their conversation overheard, especially with London flitting in and out.

"How are we going to tell her, Miguel?" asked Johann.

"Just be straightforward," replied Miguel, patting Johann's hand.

Kirt said, "I know this is rough on you, Joey. But Miguel is right. You just have to tell her."

"What if she is overjoyed with the prospect of donating organs for her OH? I can't even fathom how horrible this could be."

We have to respect her view," Kirt said. "You will have to stay objective. You can't just project your values on her, bro."

"But I can't stop this feeling that she is different. I can't put my finger on it yet, but I just know she's not like the rest, even Abby, Miguel. They both are different."

"I don't know about that," said Kirt. "Maybe you're projecting your desires and wishes on this relationship."

Miguel suddenly looked at both of them. His eyes were wide as if a light bulb had just turned on. "Oh my God, Johann. I may be as nuts as you, but I think I have seen that too. I confused it with my wishful thinking. I swear when I greeted Abby with my usual kiss on both cheeks, she actually blushed. And that look in her eyes. True clones wouldn't blush, would they Johann?"

"Man, you guys," said Kirt. "I guess you're going to have to pursue these observations," as he punched them both in the arm.

"Well I am a physician. I will interview them from a medical perspective under the guise of scientific study. I mean, that's really what my job is with the clone population anyway, right?"

"Exactly," piped in Miguel, nodding in agreement.

Johann's mind was racing and his heart pounding. "You know they have made great strides in developing the human's ability to regenerate their own parts. Since 2010, they have been working steadily to speed up the creation of specialized cells to repair damaged ones. They don't need fetal byproduct stem cells for this either, anymore." They could see the excitement building in Johann as he spoke.

"What are you getting at, Johann?" asked Miguel, seeing a change in Johann's demeanor.

"I foresee never needing to create clones for the purpose of organ donation. We are on the brink of this new scientific evolution. Somehow we must stop the creation of these precious people. Humans have no idea or even care about their clones. But now that we have been inside their world, we have a whole new perspective."

"Wow," said Miguel. "This is a pretty big task you're contemplating. I'm not even sure we or our successors can do anything about this. Humans are too used to having their lifesavers at their fingertips. It is too easy for them."

"But if we soon have other ways to do the same thing, morally we have to stop this barbaric practice," protested Johann.

"The problem is, Johann, humans want instant cures. If they have to rely on their own cell regeneration, it takes a while. Meanwhile, they are suffering or run the risk of succumbing to their disease before their body can make new parts. After donating a part, clones can regenerate their own replacement part in just three to four days. A human cannot do that. Sure, they can grow more liver, if part of it is removed, but they certainly don't do that very quickly." Miguel was trying to be supportive of Johann, but he was also realistic. He reached over and picked up the coffee carafe and poured more coffee into the cups of Kirt and Johann.

"That's a huge problem," added Kirt. "We humans are very selfish and self-serving.

"But, the clones never get these diseases or physical problems like humans. Why can't we teach humans to live a healthy lifestyle and prevent theses scourges in the first place?"

"Well, there we have it," said Kirt with a shrug. "Already we are trying to change the world."

"First things first," Miguel said with a huge sigh. "The problem at hand is talking with Peyton."

"I know. But I am just so disturbed with this whole thing. Humans have a better chance of long life now anyway with such advancements in living conditions. No pollution, and we have healthier plants and vegetables since chemicals are no longer used. Governments are trying to continue to preserve our earth by reducing over-crowding, sending four billion people to inhabit planet Gliese, one of the planets named after, and circling the star of the same name, as well as providing all kinds of exercise opportunities. But most of the humans don't take advantage of the advances made for their well-being. They can prevent or reverse many of their physical health problems and never need their clone."

Kirt leaned in across the table and asked Johann, "So do you think any of us will someday use our own clone?"

They all looked at each other with profound anguish. "Oh my God," blurted out Johann, "how can we now? What once was totally acceptable is now barbaric to me. These are people. Caring, productive, maybe even loving people."

"We have clones," said Miguel, shaking his head. "I never really gave much thought to having an exact copy of myself somewhere. I mean, I knew one existed, but I, like everyone, just assumed they were in large tanks. The work was so classified that even I was not privy to its details."

"It's pretty mind-boggling," said Kirt.

"Now that I have seen this community," continued Miguel. "I am overwhelmed." He paused and looked into Johann's eyes. "You are right, Johann. Our overall new objective must be to abolish this practice."

"In the meantime, we still need to make their lives as fulfilling as possible, world-wide. This community seems not to have any obvious problems with their lifestyle," said Johann.

Just then London bounced in, pouring one more round of coffee. "Abby just called and you need to wrap it up soon. She and Peyton are heading home. Wine is awaiting you."

The guys smiled broadly at the thought of going to their home for a cozy, intimate evening. "You got it, London." Kirt said. "We are about done anyway," as he glanced at the other two. They all nodded.

Their discussion was over for now. They were going to enjoy the evening and wonderful dinner.

As they were walking out, Johann whispered to Miguel, "I am going to get Peyton aside to approach the subject of not only my observations and concerns, but also inform her of what's looming in her future. What if she blows me off? What if I can't get her permission to scientifically evaluate her?"

"Johann, you are very persuasive. You'll convince her. I have more faith in you than you do." He flung his arm over Johann's shoulders and shook him in a brotherly embrace.

"I sure hope you're right, mi amigo. Sure hope you're right," as he slipped into the waiting car.

CHAPTER 17

Claire, Barron, and their other housemates, Harper and Graham, had the dinner well underway. Since Abby's call at 10:00 am they had plenty of time to prepare a wonderful fare. The menu included vegan beef with ginger (imitation beef steaks sautéed with ginger and scallions over jasmine rice) and a medley of root vegetables with fresh herbs of coriander and thyme. There were a variety of other side dishes of spring rolls, squired faux chicken and sweet potato casserole with crushed pecans and dried agave sugar topping. Prior to this course, they would have Claire's exquisite soup and a multi-leaf salad.

"I don't think they'll go away hungry, Clair," joked Barron, as he placed the silverware on the table.

"I want them to have a good sampling of our delicious food, Barron. Who knows how long they will be here this time, so I want to cram in as much as I can," she laughed.

Their six-year-old twins were helping set the table, putting the knives, forks and spoons in their designated spot as they had been taught. The baby was babbling in the swing, happy to be watching all the activity around her. Harper and Graham were making the salads and keeping an eye on Claire's soup. Their four kids were on sleepovers with friends and would be back the next afternoon. They all loved to entertain and were so excited about having special guests.

The large table in the expansive dining room was adorned with a white tablecloth with gold threads woven through it. There were glass candleholders of varying heights holding beautiful white candles with festive fall ribbons around each one. In the middle of the candles, a brilliant centerpiece of fresh flowers of mums, sunflowers and berries perfectly accentuated the crisp fall theme. The exquisite white, gold-rimmed china with matching salad plates and soup bowls, finished off the look with a touch of elegance. The white cloth napkins were clasped with napkin rings of fall flowers affixed to gold rings.

Claire surveyed the table to make sure it was just right. "Barron, honey, please bring in the salt and pepper shakers. The table looks awesome," she announced, pleased with the display. "Great job, all you helpers," as she grabbed both twins and squeezed them hard. They both beamed with delight and hugged their mom. "Okay, you two, you can scat," as she directed them toward their bedroom. They had eaten and were just as glad to be able to hang out in their room while the grownups had their fancy-schmancy dinner party.

It was getting cold outside, so Barron had a cozy fire going in the living room fireplace. It also opened to the dinning room, adding warmth and ambiance.

Suddenly, the door swung open, Abby and Peyton came bouncing in, followed by Johann and Miguel. Kirt and London would wait for Andre as he parked the car.

"Hey, you guys," yelled Abby, "thanks so much for preparing our dinner. It smells wonderful." She and Peyton had waited for the guys on the front porch, arriving only minutes before them

The guys sniffed the air, taking in the fabulous aroma coming from the kitchen. "We are in for a feast, I predict," said Miguel as he slipped off his jacket and headed toward the kitchen. Claire came around the corner with a bottle of wine and a handful of wine glasses, the long stems wedged between her fingers. Johann pulled off his jacket and hurried over to help Claire with the glasses.

"Here, let me get some of those," he said as he managed to get a few out of her hand without dropping them. "Yum, more of that local delicious wine, I see," he commented with a wide smile.

"We have good vineyards for sure," Claire replied. "We are so glad to share it with you. In fact, we have a few bottles for you all to take back with you." She already had the cork popped and proceeded to pour each a glassful, including one for herself.

Kirt, Andre and London walked in, ditching their jackets as they joined the group. "Don't forget us," protested London. Her green eyes sparkled as she giggled. She had her arm snuggly around Kirt's, pulling him close to her. Claire poured them each a glass. London raised her glass. "Here's to a wonderful night with our new best friends. We won't hold it against them that they are humans!" They all roared and raised their glasses in response.

Miguel came back from the kitchen smacking his lips; obviously he had been given a preview of what was to come. Claire handed him a glass of wine and all clanged their glasses in a toast again.

Barron came in and announced, "Dinner is ready." He gestured with his arm very dramatically, but jokingly, for all to follow him.

"Okay, let's eat," said Claire as she led them to the dining room. She did not seat anyone, but they naturally paired off, inevitably and not surprisingly. Kirt and London were busily chatting so sat together. Abby and Miguel sat next to each other as well as Johann and Peyton. Andre, Claire, Harper and Graham filled in the other chairs. Barron, though, popped up to serve the soup and salad.

The kids were now in their rooms, ready for bed and quietly reading, the baby in her crib, sound asleep. "We have such wonderful children," Claire announced proudly. "Harper and Graham's are equally adorable," she added.

Johann thought it was amazing how the families were so humanlike, even though the children were not their biological issues, but created and placed with them. The love was so evident. So they did posses some aspects of emotion. Taking a spoonful of soup, he suddenly said, "This soup is incredible."

"It's Claire's specialty," replied Barron. "She comes up with more soup ideas."

"Thank you for your compliment," Claire responded, ladling more soup into his bowl. "Barron does a mean tofu dish, though. You must stay long enough to sample that. I hope you guys don't miss your pork and beef too much."

"Hell no," blurted out Kirt. "This food is amazing."

"That's good bud," said London. "I'm sure the cows that have been dying for you are grateful. In fact, cows have been doing their best to kill you for centuries with their artery-clogging saturated fat."

They all laughed. "Yeah, those murderers," piped in Johann.

After they finished their soup and salad, Barron cleared the dishes and proceeded to serve the main course. The guys simultaneously looked at each other in disbelief.

Miguel said, "This is as good as any New York City top restaurant. I don't know how you do it. If this is what vegetarianism consists of,

I'm converting. Those pigs will have a reprieve too," he proclaimed.

More wine was passed and lots of chatter and laughter went on for two hours. After the equally delicious dessert was consumed, they now sat at the table sipping coffee.

Johann got up to help Peyton clear the table. Claire, Barron, Harper and Graham were already putting the dirty dishes in the gigantic dishwasher. They also had a separate dishwasher just for the pots and pans. They had an assembly line going, so cleanup was rapid.

"I guess they have everything pretty much done," said Peyton to Johann. "Let's go relax in the living room." The others were still talking and laughing at the dining room table.

He was glad of her suggestion, as he really wanted to be alone with her. She led the way into the large living room. There were several areas with intimate furniture groupings. She chose the one closest to the fireplace, her delicate face illuminated by the glow of the fire.

Johann could not keep his eyes off of her. Her brown, thick hair with soft curls fell over her shoulders, framing her face. He could smell the wonderful scent of a fragrance unfamiliar to him. It was extraordinary. How could he approach her with what he had to tell? Before he could open his mouth, she asked, "Since you are a doctor and specialize in clones, I have a medical question to ask, Johann."

"Okay," he said, very curious.

Johann, I have been noticing things about myself, and Abby too." She was twirling her hair around her finger, eyes downcast.

"What kind of things, Peyton?' he asked, as he sat down next to her, studying her even more intently now.

"You know clones don't age after twenty years old, but I am seeing very odd things appearing. Now I don't know if you call it aging per se…"

"What have you noticed?" he asked as he started looking at her more carefully.

"My eyes…or rather the outer edges of my eyes," she stammered. "I see like tiny wrinkles, especially when I frown or smile. I didn't have them a few years ago and now…" again, she trailed off.

"I see," responded Johann, now really curious. He touched her forehead and temples. She looked like a beautiful twenty-something to him.

"Another thing," she went on, staring at him, almost forgetting what she wanted to say. "I get these strange feelings that I can't explain. I mean, when you look at me, or touch me...I don't know what's happening to me. I feel weak, my heart pounds, I want you close to me, and I know it is wrong. What is wrong with me?" she pleaded with him.

Johann wanted to take her in his arms and comfort her. It took all that he had to resist and keep his professional veneer. "Peyton, I think you're displaying emotions. Human emotions, but I don't understand why either. Would you mind if I do a few tests on you tomorrow?" Now his own suspicions were being verified.

"Not at all," she said. "I have felt different for a long time. I've never said anything to anyone."

"That's probably wise." He was hoping no one else suspected what he did.

"Oh, except for Abby," she remembered. "We talked about it for the first time just the other day. Strangely, she also has been experiencing some of the same symptoms. You know, much of this did not come to light until your visit!! You human brats! What have you done to us?" she teased, laughing nervously.

Oh, Peyton, if you only knew, he thought. It's not only what I am doing to you. It's what you're doing to me. This was very curious, though, she and Abby both experiencing non-clone-like features.

"Peyton, I have to tell you something." He really did not want to have this discussion, but saw no way out of it. She had to know what was most likely coming up.

"What is it?" asked Peyton, seeing alarm in Johann's eyes.

"It's your OH. She's having some medical problems and I suspect she will be requesting organs from you." He paused and waited to see her reaction.

It was not one of willing acceptance, the usual clone response. He studied her intently and was surprised, in fact, thrilled with what he saw.

"Johann, this is terrible news," she whispered. "I told you, I felt different from the others. I don't understand it, but I just don't feel excited about helping my OH. It's never felt right to me. I had always hoped I'd have a healthy OH and she would never need me." Tears were welling up in her eyes.

"It's okay, Peyton. I will help you. We'll figure it out. I promise."

"Wait," she said suddenly. "How did you know about my OH? Do you know her?" She stared into his eyes, totally dumbfounded.

"That's another story, Peyton. You don't need to worry about that right now." He dreaded having to tell her about Caitlyn. He looked away feeling so awful about his last two months with Caitlyn. He knew he would have to tell her someday, but now was not the time. He took Peyton's hand in his, looked straight into her eyes and assured her he was there for her. The fire was lapping around the large logs, and the heat was so comforting. Peyton, curled up on the couch, leaned against Johann, feeling his warm body. She felt protected and safe. Johann put his arm around her, dropping his doctor veneer now.

"Johann," she said gazing at the fire. "I don't want to do it." It surprised her as much as him.

"I understand, Peyton," he responded softly.

"I don't think you do, Johann. Since I feel I am different, what if I don't have the same regeneration properties? Can you test for that?"

"Oh my God, Peyton. I never even thought about that. I mean I really selfishly did not want you having to undergo the procedure for many reasons, but I had no reason to worry about your regeneration capability." He sounded almost panicked now. He sat her up and took her by both shoulders and looked straight into her fearful eyes. "Tomorrow I will test you for that. It's a genetic test and I can get immediate results."

"Okay. I have to know. I understand I am being very unclone-like, saying I don't wish to sacrifice my life for my OH," tears now rolling down her cheeks.

"Peyton, there is no way I will let that happen," exclaimed Johann. "If I have to hide you...," as he said it, the idea became real. My God, he was thinking. I may have to get her out of here and hide her. But where and how? His mind was reeling. But first he had to test her. He had to know.

Peyton then said, softy, lips trembling, "Johann, you have to test Abby too. You know we were birthed at the same time, at the same facility. Knowing us, our tanks were probably side by side," she said with a half-forced smile.

Johann knew he would need to investigate their records. He needed to see if there had been any irregularity and find out who their lab techs were. He would get Kirt on that detail in the morning.

He took her face in his hands. "Peyton, I promise I will look after you. No matter what. She dissolved into his arms, tears now flowing freely. He loved her. He was sure of it. He had from the moment he laid eyes on her. He was going to have to save her life.

Not only for her, but for him.

CHAPTER 18

They had ended their evening around 11:00 pm and were directed to a home nearby that was readied for them. It consisted of a five-bedroom, beautifully decorated home that was used for housing visitors from various clone communities and local administrators who came for conferences.

At 6:00 am, Johann was already up, heading out the door to do a half-hour run. He had slept fitfully, knowing the following day was going to be difficult. Before they retired, he had clued the guys in on his conversation with Peyton. Kirt already had lab equipment brought on board their jet. He was always prepared for the unknown-that was Kirt.

By the time Johann returned from his run, the kitchen was amassed with people preparing a feast of a breakfast. Kirt, Andre and Miguel were up and dressed, sipping the exquisite coffee. "Hey," shouted Johann, as he raced up the steps to the second floor. "Give me ten minutes and I'll be down to join you."

After a quick shower and shave, he met them in the kitchen. He was dressed in heavy jeans, brown turtleneck and a cashmere, diamond-design, crew neck sweater. Kirt and Andre both were in blue jeans and heavy sweaters, prepared for the cold day that was predicted. Miguel, likewise, was in a charcoal-gray sweater with dark-gray, corduroy pants.

Kirt said, "I've got the lab equipment set up with the computer in the den. It's calibrated and ready to go." He sat at a massive table, hardly able to contain himself in anticipation of another exceptional meal.

"Good," responded Johann, giving a sigh. "I will call the girls over after breakfast. The sooner we know, the better." He joined Kirt at the table.

"Maybe you should test some others as a control," said Miguel.

"Not a bad idea," Johann responded. "I'm sure Claire and Barron won't mind."

"Barron is living proof already, Johann," said Kirt.

"Really? How's that?" asked Johann, surprised.

"London told me he was recently a donor for his OH and regenerated just fine. By the way, he was thrilled to do it."

"Okay…so we don't have to test him, for sure."

"I think asking Graham and Harper key questions may be enough to evaluate them. But I would still like to test Claire, if she will let us."

Miguel said, "This is really going to be interesting to see if anything genetically is askew with these two."

"Kirt, have you found who the genetic engineer and technician were at the time of their creation and subsequent birthing?" Johann was still totally perplexed.

"Yessiree, I have. His name is Dr. Ken Bronson. He was a young researcher at the time, very knowledgeable and well respected. He's around fifty-two now and working out of the Arizona Research Lab."

"Let's Skype him after our test results," said Johann. "He may remember if there was anything unusual happening that day twenty-eight years ago." Johann's face now contorted with a worried look.

The breakfast was outstanding, not surprisingly. They wasted no time gulping it down though, as they wanted to get to their task ahead. They needed to do blood work to determine metabolic rates, and hormone levels and a regeneration-specific genes test. It was 8 o'clock already. The phone suddenly rang, startling them. Johann jumped up to answer it.

"Hey, are you guys up and at 'em?" asked a seemingly wide-awake Peyton.

"Sure are. I even got a half hour run in."

"You stinker. You should have called us. We would have joined you."

"It was pretty early, Peyton. I didn't want to disturb your beauty sleep."

"We're early risers. Tomorrow we'll definitely go with you. We'll see what you are made of through the steep paths that Abs and I take."

"Great. Go easy on this old boy," he laughed

"So, are we on for this morning?" she inquired.

"Yup. We have things set up here if you want to come now."

"OK. We'll be on our way."

He hung up the phone and looked at Miguel and Kirt. "So I guess we will have our answers soon." They all just sat there looking pretty glum.

"Okay, my friends. We have to not show our concern to these girls," said Johann. They all agreed to put on their smiles.

"Johann, has there been any formal request for organ donation for Caitlyn?" asked Miguel.

"Kirt?" asked Johann.

"No, not yet," replied Kirt as he headed into the den. "I'll check on her health status again. As of yesterday, she had been hospitalized twenty-four hours. They were still working her up and things did not look good. Her liver was failing and her heart failure advancing too. I'm sure the request is imminent."

"Miguel, we have to get Peyton out of here regardless of the test results," pleaded Johann. "She doesn't have the mindset of typical clones and doesn't want to participate, even if she possesses the ability to regenerate."

"Kirt, work on a logistical plan. You can take the upstairs library to use your laptop. Andre can work out the frequencies and jamming devices for the jet. Kirt, we need the codes for the personal GPS integral jamming procedures too. I know mine, as obviously I have to use it often in my world travels," said Miguel. "Johann, you must have yours and Kirt's handy too, right?"

"Certainly, but we will need the codes for Peyton," he said. "And in case Abby wants to go, we need one for her," he added.

"One for London too," said Kirt.

They both looked at him.

"What? Why are you staring at me? Maybe she wants to tag along," throwing his arms in the air.

"Kirt, we don't even know where we are going. We can't be sure any of them will want to take off and hide."

"Well, Andre and I will look at our options and get back to you," he said as they both scrambled up the stairs.

They heard a tap on the front door. It sprang open with Peyton and Abby in their usual chipper mood bounding into the entranceway.

"Good morning," they chirped in unison.

Johann and Miguel jumped to their feet to greet them warmly.

"Abby wants to be tested too," Peyton announced before poor Abby had a chance to explain.

"Peyton, you could have waited for me to tell them," whined Abby.

"Abby, we were kind of hoping you'd agree to also be tested," said Johann as he pulled out a chair for Peyton, then her. "This is a critical thing, girls, and you can't take this lightly. You know this is going to impact your life and your future," he warned.

As giddy as they appeared, the girls knew they were just trying to play down the significance of the outcome of these tests. But as reality was sinking in and the enormous consequence now weighing on their minds, they became very quiet.

They then hugged each other. Abby spoke first. "Peyton, my loving, adorable sister, no matter what, we will face this together. We are so very thankful to Johann and Miguel for entering our lives and probably saving them too. We are not going to change who we are or let this depress us or defeat us." She stuck her chin up in the air, defiantly.

Peyton, now with tears in her eyes said, "Abby, you have always been my strength. You have always had my back, and we will always have each other no matter what lies ahead. Let's get this done. Now!" She looked at Johann and Miguel, not with fear but with sheer determination.

"Alright then, let's do it." Johann pointed to the large den.

Peyton, pulling off her jacket, said, "I'll go first, Abby," as she made her way out of the kitchen and headed to the makeshift lab.

Abby, not to be left behind, scurried after her, wrapping her arms around her chest. "I'm coming too, sister."

It was just a matter of minutes and they both had had their blood drawn. Kirt and Andre appeared at the doorway and asked, "Do you need any help with the chemometer? I have it calibrated so it should be ready."

"Sure," replied Johann. "Help me set up the specimens for the gene comparisons. Here, do this one," as he handed Kirt a labeled vial of blood. They had the slides set up in no time. The girls sat immobile, watching intently. Miguel was standing beside them with his hands on each of their shoulders.

"Let's not be so melodramatic," said Peyton, as the room became deathly silent. "It's gotten awfully serious in here," as she tried to lighten the mood.

Johann looked up trying desperately not to show his deep concern and anxiety. The slides were completed and ready for insertion into the machine. The genes would be deciphered and chromosomes examined for any missing links. They would know soon if these blood samples were atypical in any way. The genetic manipulation that was responsible for the triple regeneration factor would be immediately identifiable if it were present. If it were not present, then something obviously went terribly wrong at the time of the original creation of the fetus.

Peyton's report came back first: NO GENETIC COMPONENT FOR TRIPLE REGENERATION.

Johann just stared at the printout. He could not even find the words to report the findings to Peyton. Abby's came up within seconds: NO GENETIC COMPONENT FOR TRIPLE REGENERATION. Johann had to sit back down.

"Johann, what is it?" asked Miguel, sensing a problem.

"Ahhh," stuttered Johann. I just have to do one more test on each of the girls." Peyton, please come over here and sit down in this chair. I will be putting a helmet-like apparatus on your head. Don't worry, it won't hurt me a bit." He tried to hide his extreme anxiousness.

"Very funny, mister."

This instrument would calibrate the brain waves and determine the amount of manipulation to the frontal lobe that was supposedly done following the birthing of the clone. There were set parameters for the procedure that could then be observed by this particular instrument in the event repeat manipulation needed to be done. Very rarely was this needed, but on rare occasions it was known that a clone, here and there, needed to return for this tweaking and/or be disposed of.

Peyton was nervous now, especially after seeing Johann's reaction to her blood test results.

"Just hold very still now, Peyton" instructed Johann. He was watching the screen and pushing buttons expertly. Within a few minutes Johann let out a "hmmm.

Okay I think I am done here. Abby, your turn."

Peyton rose to her feet feeling a little light-headed. This was bothering her more than she had anticipated.

Abby slid into the seat now. "Beam me up, Scotty," she giggled.

"Oh Abs," complained Peyton. "You never worry about anything. I so envy you."

"Aw, Peyton. You just have to chill out. What's the big deal?"

After a few minutes and more button pushing, Johann was done. So there it was. The results were in. Abby and Peyton now squirmed in their seats, getting antsy.

"Johann, please tell us," cried out the girls at once.

" Abby, Peyton. You are both clones. That's a given. You were created in a lab from original humans. But here's the catch. Neither of you has the triple regeneration factor." He continued. "Okay, here's the deal. Properties that were supposed to be genetically engineered into you are absent. In addition, neither of you had the frontal lobe of your brain altered as is the normal procedure. I don't know if this is going to be good news or bad for you."

Miguel, Kirt and Andre stood there in total disbelief and shock. The girls were staring at Johann with their mouths wide open, looking back and forth to everyone

Johann continued, "You both are perfect specimens with all the genetic properties of humans. Exact copies. That's why you are feeling strange desires and attitudes. They are unclone-like, for sure. Those are human qualities that are supposed to be tweaked out of clone creations. You two somehow slipped through the cracks."

Abby and Peyton just sat there totally numb. Abby finally responded, "But why, how, what happened?"

"I don't have an answer for that, Abby, but Kirt is looking into it. He already has the name and location of the researcher who was involved at the time of your creation and birth. We will get to the bottom of this."

"What about London?" asked Peyton, still very shaken. "Do you think she could also be like us?"

"Why do you ask? Has she questioned anything or expressed any concerns?" asked Miguel.

"Well, no, not exactly. It's just that she is just as outspoken and crazy as us and just not a typical clone, you know, subservient and accepting."

"Well, we can test her too, if she's willing," said Johann.

"Oh my God, how do we even approach her with this?" said Abby. "She may think we are all loony."

Kirt broke in. "Let me break it to her. We sort of have a pretty good friendship. Let me feel her out."

"Okay then," said Johann. "Why don't you do that now. Meanwhile, we all need to make some immediate plans about where we go from here." Abby and Peyton just starred at him, then at each other.

Kirt disappeared briefly then reappeared with a phone in his hand. "I've got Dr. Branson on the phone, Joey."

Johann took the phone. "Yes, Dr. Bronson, I understand you were involved with clone operations and birthing at the New York facility in June of 2037. I need to ask you some questions surrounding a particular day. I am hoping you can remember some details."

"Certainly, Dr. Christiansen, I can try. What is the date?"

"It was June 27, 2037. As you know, I am the Director of the International Clone Federation, and we are in the process of doing random testing of clones from different time periods. Just routine." He winked at Peyton. He certainly did not want to set off any alarms.

"Sure, okay," he replied.

"Were there any unusual events or problems with the cloning process on that date?" Johann inquired.

"Wow, that was a long time ago. But I can tell you I did have some irregularities occur. I think it was around then. I had never seen such a thing. But it was like one type of cells just did not want to cooperate. It was like a rogue cell. It just would not comply with the usual genetic pairing. But the babies formed, so I didn't abort them. I just thought I would let them grow and recheck to make sure all was well. They seemed fine and perfect fetal specimens. They thrived and I actually forgot all about them. You know we were creating and birthing thousands."

"What about the brain-lobe tweaking to assure the clone compliance?" asked Johann.

That was weird too. It was done, but again, it was like the cells kept repairing themselves, not allowing the manipulation to last. Again, with so many in line, I just passed them on, feeling assured they would be disposed of at the following step."

"Hmmm, do you think there are others that may have slipped through the quality control? Not only at that facility but others too?"

"I have no idea. There never has been any talk about it or anything written in the literature, before or after. I just shucked it off as a one-time fluke. Why these questions? Is there a problem with a clone?" Now he was getting too suspicious. But since he was derelict in his duty to abort any abnormal clone, he probably was not about to make any mention of it to anyone.

"No. No problem." He did not want to explain anything and hope this doc would not be asking any questions. "That's about it. I appreciate your information."

"Sure, anytime, Dr. Christiansen. To tell you the truth, I had forgotten all about the incident. That crazy rogue cell just was not to be stopped.

CHAPTER 19

Peyton was still in shock over the test results. Her world had suddenly been turned upside down. From the day these humans arrived in their community, something in her gut told her things were about to change. She had had no idea what was about to come.

Suddenly the front door flew open and in popped London. She was dressed in a pastel, teal, cashmere, jumpsuit with leather boots up to mid-thigh. "Hey people, starting a real early party without me, huh? Gee, if it weren't for Kirt calling me, I wouldn't be here joining the festivities." She feigned hurt, pouting. She did a double take at the somber faces staring back at her. "What's up with you guys? You look like someone died. I know it's early, but please cheer up." She continued to watch them. "Come on, you're scaring me."

She was interrupted by the voice of Kirt, who was busily working with the computer and so entranced he did not even notice her arrival. "I've scoped it out." Miguel was by his side observing the maps Kirt was bringing up to the screen. "We can go to Sweden. Kirun-it's a small, remote village in the north. I have people who can hide you. It's the easiest to get to undetected, too. Over the arctic."

"Hello to you too," she said as they didn't even acknowledge her. Kirt threw a hand in the air as a greeting.

Without missing a beat, Miguel nodded. "Sounds good, Kirt. You can then drop me off in France. No one will associate me with your disappearance. No one knew I was going with you to Community 27."

"That's true, Mikie. We just kind of smuggled you out," Kirt said with a wide grin.

"My people think I'm in my New York apartment not wanting to be disturbed for a few days. My cell phone is scrambled anyway. No one can determine my location."

"Great perk of being president of the whole world," quipped Abby. She was looking from face to face trying to be as upbeat as possible. Truth was, she had great concerns about their impending escape.

"Yup," responded Miguel. "Just remember, you all will NOT be able to use your cell phones whatsoever." He was still looking at the computer screen, studying the maps with Kirt. Abby got a big, sad look with her bottom lip over her upper, like a disappointed five-year old girl. Miguel looked up and laughed. "Awww, come on, Abby, it can't be that bad."

"Are you kidding, Miguel?" she protested. "I use my cell phone apps for everything just to get through the day!"

Peyton now joined her. "That's where we get our recipes, keep track of our tasks… ah, I guess we won't be needing them after all. Since we are going to be in hiding on an arctic tundra, does that mean we have to subsist on whale meat? I feel sick already." She feigned regurgitation. "Okay, but we can bring our e-readers, right?"

"No!" responded Miguel. Anything hi-tech will not be used except for Johann and Kirt's cell phones, which are especially designed to be scrambled.

Peyton really was disappointed now. "Well, can I at least bring an old-fashioned, hard-cover book?"

"You could, but we don't have time to stop at the library for you to pick one up. We'll find something to occupy you gals."

Peyton now laughed, but underneath she was scared to death. Her very life depended on a successful escape.

Johann looked away from the computer screen. "Peyton, I'm so sorry we can't let you go anywhere, not to your office, your home, anywhere.

Abby and Peyton stared at him in disbelief. "We can't even say good-bye to Claire, Barron and our family?" asked Peyton.

"Sorry, no. No one. They know you are here, but they are not going to know you are gone from the community. Not for a few days, I hope."

London, listening to all this with her mouth wide open, asked, "Am I included in this, ah, escape? I don't want to be left behind, you guys, even though I don't have the vaguest idea of what's going on here."

"Yes, London, you are going." Johann nodded as he stood up to face all of them. They would have to test her later as their equipment had been packed by Andre and ready to be stowed in the waiting car. "You all are going with the clothes on your back, too. We have warm sweaters, pants and long underwear on board for all."

Kirt joined in. "You will take no ID. Your imbedded chips will be scrambled, so you cannot be GPS'd. The transponder and avionics of the aircraft will also be scrambled so that our flight will be undetectable."

Johann continued. "You will call Claire and tell her you both have an urgent matter in Oneonta to take care of and will probably be gone overnight and up to three days, if necessary. If she asks about clothes, just tell her you have a change of clothes at the office that you are taking. Also tell her we headed back to New York City."

Miguel added, "Since there is no communication between you and the humans anyway, once they miss you, it will only be known in this community. No other human is allowed in here under any circumstance. Only your community representative would be allowed to go out to talk, if it comes to that. Since I will be going to France, there will be continuity of my duties."

"I won't be missed that much," said Johann. "They are used to my being MIA occasionally, right Kirt?"

Kirt nodded and rolled his eyes.

"Hopefully, nothing will be noticeably askew as far as the human world goes until a possible organ request and the clone does not come forward. That will prompt a demand for an explanation," said Kirt.

"By then," Johann added, "We will be securely hidden in our remote Shangri-La."

"Shangri-La, indeed," groaned Peyton. "Okay, I get it. But once they find I am not responding to their request, what is their procedure?" Peyton was now nervously pacing.

Johann stopped her, taking her head in his hands and looking directly into her tear-filled eyes.

"Peyton, I can't lie to you. They will command your people to search every square inch of the community. Your people are loyal to you, I know, but their DNA and brains will override their devotion to you. They will have to find you and turn you over to your own authorities. They will not care about your plight either."

Miguel asked, "Has this ever happened before, Peyton? Where someone refused to be a donor?"

"Never to my knowledge." She was visibly flustered at the thought of her friends hunting her down.

"You know, Peyton, they have no idea you are different. They may think that you have had an accident with your computer-operated vehicle and somehow went off the road into a ravine. But believe me, they won't leave a stone unturned in looking for you."

Kirt added, "They may not put together our visit with your disappearance. Remember, you are going to tell Claire we already left and that you, Abby and London are taking off immediately, and by yourselves, for Oneonta."

Johann then encircled Peyton with his arms, and she snuggled into his body. He held her tightly as she cried softly. "Peyton, it's going to be alright. I will protect you. Miguel will be in France, in view, and able to monitor what's going on. He'll be able to keep us informed."

Abby then stood up, put her hands on her hips and said. "Why don't I go with Miguel? Hmmm, a trip to France." She smiled dreamily.

"Abby, are you crazy?" Miguel and Johan cried in unison.

"No one knows me and after all, I am a pretty good copy of a human." She threw her hands in the air and did a swirl.

"Absolutely not! You will stay under the radar with your sister and London." Johann gave her a half-smile. At least it stopped Peyton's tears as she laughed and cried at the same time.

Johann extended Peyton to arm's length. She was so beautiful and loving, and he knew he would do whatever necessary to protect her, even if it meant losing his position in the world's government or losing his life. She was now his world.

CHAPTER 20

Cardiac monitors beeped to her heart rate. Caitlyn, the reigning queen of fashion, lay there with multiple IVs, two central lines, two peripheral lines with triple-port lumens, all with life-saving medication flowing into her failing body. A nasal cannula delivered oxygen at four liters per minute, indicating her lung function was declining. She clearly was in trouble. She went in and out of consciousness as powerful sedative drugs were administered to alleviate her pain, restlessness, and frequent combativeness.

"I don't think we can reverse things here," said Dr. Dan Conrad. He was the top cardiologist at New York City Metropolitan Health Center, an acute care hospital with state-of-the art technologies and the most outstanding specialists in the United States.

Dr. Ed Burns, a nephrologist, looked at Caitlyn, shaking his head. "Dan, you've done everything possible." He studied the latest ultrasound test in his hand. "I think it's time to replace her failing organs. They're beyond recovery at this point. Her kidneys are shutting down. To buy us some time, I have ordered dialysis. They're setting up the equipment as we speak."

"Then I concur, Ed. I will get the ball rolling and put in the request for her clone organs to be harvested immediately. She's gone downhill so rapidly and unexpectedly. We don't even have time to give the clone a few days to prepare for the procedure. But emergencies do happen from time to time, and I am quite confident that this should be no problem for the clone procurement team."

Dr Burns closed the chart he had been studying, sliding it under his arm. "I will go ahead and schedule the OR for tomorrow, mid-morning. You contact the clone representative and have Caitlyn's clone in their hospital tonight, ready for harvesting early tomorrow morning."

"Sounds good. We'll have the transplant team ready with the helicopter on the roof of the clone hospital, ready to receive the organs. Dr. Conrad studied her EKG on the monitor. "Her heart is struggling and I just hope the drugs can keep it going through the night. Otherwise, I may have to put a heart pump in temporarily until we can get her new heart in place tomorrow."

"I'll call John to join the surgical team," said Dr. Burns. "He's an expert with livers. He may only have to supplement her liver with a small piece of donor liver. He will know how extensive the permanent damage is. I will call him in on consultation immediately." Dr Burns was very concerned about Caitlyn's condition. He looked at her monitor values, down at her again, and shrugged his shoulders. This one is going to be a close call. I can't believe how quickly she deteriorated. He pulled her bottom eyelids down and observed the yellow color indicating worsening liver function.

"Caitlyn, can you hear me, sweetheart?" He was very distressed over her increasing lack of responsiveness. She began to rouse, and then opened her eyes.

Dr. Conrad leaned in. "Caitlyn, you are very sick, but we're going to do everything we can to help you." She nodded, desperately trying to keep her eyes open. "We have ordered the harvesting of organs from your clone and will be transplanting them tomorrow. You have to stay strong and hang in there. Keep fighting, Cait. You can do this."

She seemed to brighten up some, and they knew Caitlyn Sarantino would muster every bit of fight she had in her to stay alive long enough for new organs to save her life.

Sarah came by the bed to check her medications and vital signs. Dr. Burns said, "Watch her like a hawk, Sarah. We'll dialyze her now, and hopefully getting some toxins out of her system will help. Call Dr. Conrad or me if anything changes. We plan to do the transplant tomorrow morning."

"I will not leave her side," Sarah promised as she was rolling Caitlyn over on her side, surrounding her with soft pillows. Caitlyn managed to squeak out two words so uncharacteristic for her. "Thank you." She knew she was in trouble this time, and her only hope was to utilize her clone and be in the hands of these highly regarded experts. Please hurry, she thought, as she drifted back into unconsciousness.

CHAPTER 21

Kirt collected all the computer and testing equipment and put them into canvas tote bags.

Johann walked Peyton over to the couch, sat her down and handed her a phone.

"Here, my dear one. Call Claire and tell her you have an emergency meeting in Oneonta but will only be gone a couple days, three at the most. And don't forget to tell her that Abby and London are needed there too. Tell her you don't have time to run home for clothes, but you have extras at the office and will grab them on your way. You have a car waiting and really can't explain details right now, but no big deal. Just a whiny administrator that needs assistance." Peyton nodded.

"And, a really big thing. Tell her Kirt, Miguel and I have left already to go back to New York City because they had an urgent deal to address."

"Okay," said Peyton, groaning. She dialed the phone, fingers trembling. She was not used to lying to her mom, but she knew she had to do it.

Miguel signaled with a two-finger salute to Johann indicating they were packed and ready to roll. Peyton finished her conversation with Claire and rose to face Johann.

"Done," she said with a sad look on her face. "She bought it. She knows how I have to handle certain top brass personally on a moments notice. It's nothing out of the ordinary for Abby and me."

"Phew," responded Johann. He once again put his hands on either side of Peyton's face and drew her to him. He lightly kissed her forehead. "We need to split now, Peyton. Don't worry. You'll be coming back, I promise you. You will." He could see her welling up again. He put his arms around her and she melted into his chest.

Miguel shouted. "Okay, amigos, time to depart. Vamanos!"

Abby and London threw on their coats and headed out, followed by Peyton and Johann, hand in hand. As soon as the last one had their seat belt buckled, Andre threw the car in gear and had them speeding toward the airport.

He already had prepared the jet hours ago, so it was fueled and ready to go on their arrival. Andre jumped aboard to go down the checklist. The rest departed the car and boarded the plane within minutes. Kirt then drove the car and deposited it near the FBO and threw the keys to the attendant. There was no view of the plane from where they were standing, so there was no witnessing of the girls entering it.

"See ya later, Ben," Kirt said over his shoulder to the attendant. "We have to scoot back to New York. Unexpected work awaits us," he said with a laugh.

"Okay, buddy, see you again soon."

"You bet," answered Kirt. He loped back to the plane, brought up the stairs behind him and latched the door. Andre had already completed the preflight check and powered up the engines. He hopped into the left-side pilot seat. He looked over his shoulder to the group in the cabin and said, "We're all set guys so hold onto your hats. This is going to be an outstanding ride.

Peyton started to apologize profusely, citing all the danger and inconvenience she was causing, when they all cut her off. "Peyton," Kirt said. "You are worth every bit of this adventure. Think of it as a winter holiday," he laughed. He was heading the jet down the taxiway to the runway.

Miguel and Johann joined in. "Peyton, you are so loved by everyone. Your clone friends, family and us, especially Johann." She quickly looked over at Johann, who was watching her with incredibly adoring eyes.

"And you know, after this escapade is over," said Johann," the whole world will know you and love you too."

Miguel smiled at her adoringly too. Abby and London got up and hugged her.

"Okay, okay," shouted Kirt. "Back to your seats. We're taking off momentarily." At that, the roar of the engines escalated and they were off the ground like a bullet.

Peyton peered out the window to see her world, her community, getting smaller and smaller until it was gone from sight. She straightened up, smiled and said, "Into the future, the unknown, on an adventure of a lifetime with my friends by my side." Her fear subsided in an instant. Her world had changed, and like it or not, she would evolve as it was meant to be.

Kirt and Andre expertly aimed the aircraft for the arctic zone, having already encrypted the avionics. Johann, meanwhile, had the imbedded microchip scrambler busy at work.

His world and Peyton's were colliding. Until just a few short months ago, they were literally worlds apart. Now his safety was in jeopardy because of her. But none of that mattered. Not only were their worlds meant to cross paths, they were meant to be together, some way, somehow. He was sure of that.

CHAPTER 22

"Good morning, Dr. Conrad." Sarah was back on duty after just a few hours of sleep in a nearby room. While adjusting the IVs, she reported, "Caitlyn had a good night. The dialysis really stabilized her, thank goodness."

"That's good news, Sarah. Let me see how she responds." Dr. Conrad leaned over Caitlyn. "Caitlyn, open your eyes. Look at me, Caitlyn," he insisted. She flickered her eyelids and then opened her eyes, staring up at him. "Good girl, Cait. Now squeeze my hand as hard as you can." Caitlyn squeezed his hand as directed, but was weak at best. "Excellent," Dr. Conrad said, very pleased. "We've bought some time, Sarah. Did Dr. Burns make all the arrangements for the transplant today?" He was flipping through her chart, looking at the lab results.

"Ah, I don't think things are set, Dr. Conrad. I don't know the details. He said to have you call him." She gave him an "I'm sorry" look.

"Will do. Right now," as he snapped his cell phone off his waist with annoyance, his eyes narrowing. His patience was wearing thin.

Caitlyn, rousing more and more, seemed to be listening with some understanding.

"Hey, Ed, Dan here. What's happening with the organ transplant for Caitlyn this morning?" His forehead suddenly creased. "They haven't been able to contact the clone? Oh, I see. Okay," he said, repeatedly glancing at the clock. "Caitlyn has improved a lot, so we have some time. I will go ahead and cancel the OR for this am, but we'll keep everyone on call. The team can be assembled within an hour's notice. Let me know the minute the arrangements are finalized.

Okay. Keep me posted."

When he hung up, Sarah and Caitlyn were staring at him. "There has been a slight delay," he explained. "Apparently her clone has left for an emergency meeting a few hours away from her home. They are in the process of locating her." He could see a huge frown on Caitlyn's face. Well, at least her brain comprehended, which was a good thing. She clearly understood the circumstances. Now to keep her calm, he thought, as he could see her anxiety mounting.

Caitlyn's mind was whirling. She thought, how could a clone have meetings? What the hell? Get my parts, damn it.

"It's alright, Caitlyn. You are doing fine. There's no problem with a few hours delay. Even twenty-four is okay. You're stable. We aren't going to let anything happen to you." He patted her shoulder and looked straight into her pleading eyes. "It really is not uncommon not to find a clone on a moments notice. It's not like they're waiting in a hospital. He grinned and gave her a reassuring hug. She reached her hand to his and squeezed hard this time. As she struggled to speak, Dr. Conrad put his finger to her lips and said. "Cait, it's not a big deal, really." If only that were true.

She was desperate to tell him something and kept trying. Finally out came, "Find her, find her." She was pleading with every ounce of her strength.

"We will, Caitlyn. But you must save your strength to stay well. Don't fret," he admonished her, but with a smile. Her eyes, now sunken and dull, were closing even as she was fighting to stay awake.

"Get some rest, hon," Dr Conrad said as he surveyed her. She nodded as she once again slipped into sleep.

"Sarah, call me if anything changes. At least she's not in a coma. Just exhausted, poor thing."

Dan Conrad walked out of the room just as Dr. Burns strolled toward him. He was on his cell phone. He did not look happy as he snapped it off.

"Oh boy, Ed. What the hell is going on? Our Caitlyn is more and more aware and is pretty worried about the delay in her transplant. She's better, but certainly not out of the woods."

"I don't know what to say, Dan. They still haven't located her. The clone rep says they are concerned about what may have happened to her. It's pretty hilly with steep drop-offs along the highway where she and two other administrators were headed. They are combing the area. There's nothing we can do at this point but wait."

"Can we send in our people?" asked Dr. Conrad, really getting concerned at this point.

"Nope. Not allowed. Ever. They have capable people and resources to handle anything."

"Never? Geez."

"Well, I guess if there were a direct order from the President of the New World Order or the High Commissioner of the United States...but there would have to be a really damn big emergency. Not sure getting donor parts for an international jet-setter counts."

"Are you kidding? Caitlyn is an international star. The world would insist on every step possible if it were a matter of life and death. Besides, her father is a pretty important dude too. I'm actually surprised he is not here already." Dr. Conrad looked at his watch.

Just then, they heard the clip-clop sound of high heels coming down the hallway.

On the arm of a striking, well-dressed gentleman was a petite, stunning beauty with sable-dark hair, dark complexion and very familiar chocolate-brown eyes. Dr. Conrad looked at Ed and said, "Speak of the devil."

Caitlyn, a precocious child and beautiful from birth, was born to a socialite mother and a college professor father. Besides being a highly successful professor, her dad now was president of a very prestigious Ivy League college. He also had plenty of old money from his father, also a prominent college provost.

Dr. Sarantino had been at Harvard for almost his entire career, and he was now nearing fifty-eight years old. He was contemplating an early retirement to have time to travel and enjoy his riches and lifelong connections. He loved his career and was devoted to it. He had had a faithful administrative assistant for twenty years, though, who fulfilled his need for companionship and love that were lacking from home. He would somehow have to figure out a way of keeping her in his life should he decide to give up his career. He was deeply in love with her and could not imagine life without her in it.

Reine Sarantino, his attractive wife of twenty-nine years, had mixed emotions about his retiring. She traveled constantly with her likewise affluent gal pals, having exciting, romantic liaisons wherever she went. Her husband was wrapped up in his career so couldn't care less about her escapades, so she rationalized. She was French, constantly dividing her time between France, partying with her cousins, and Connecticut, participating in New York society affairs. Michael's retirement certainly was going to interfere with her independence, she had huffed to herself upon his announcement.

As they approached closer, the man reached his hand out to Dr. Conrad. "I'm Dr. Michael Sarantino, Caitlyn's father. This is my wife, Reine. We came as soon as we were notified. What's happening? Is our daughter okay?"

Dr. Conrad shook his hand. "It's nice to meet you. So sorry it's under these circumstances. This is Dr. Burns. He is a nephrologist, attending to your daughter." Dr. Burns shook his hand and nodded to Reine.

"Dr. Sarantino, I am a cardiologist also seeing your daughter. She is experiencing some organ failure. She is stable at the moment. We are preparing to transplant her heart, liver and possibly a kidney. She destabilized rather quickly, but we have an excellent team here and are able to maintain her functions adequately until we can complete the transplants."

"So you are planning transplant surgery today?" he asked, with sudden worry in his eyes.

"Well, we'd like to." Dr. Conrad shifted his eyes from Dr. Sarantino to his wife. Mrs. Sarantino looked distraught and was now leaning on her husband for support. She asked, her voice shaky with a growing fear, "So what is the problem? Do we have a problem?"

"It takes time, you know, to put all the pieces together. We have to round up the clone, do the harvesting and prep the recipient etcetera. It just takes some coordination." He was not about to worry them unnecessarily. He glanced over at Dr. Burns, who said, "It was nice to meet you and we will do everything possible to help your beloved daughter." He shook everyone's hand and departed, once again, reaching for his cell phone.

Dr. Conrad said, "Let me take you to Caitlyn. This way," he said, as he escorted them to Caitlyn's bedside. The ICU was enormous with a nurses' station in the center and private rooms with sliding glass doors, surrounding it. Monitors were beeping from all corners of the very busy unit. Sarah was at Caitlyn's side as usual.

"Sarah, these are Caitlyn's parents, Dr. and Mrs. Michael Sarantino," said Dr. Conrad. "Dr. Sarantino, this is the best ICU nurse on the planet."

Sarah came over and reached out with both hands to welcome them. "He exaggerates a bit," she apologized. She gave both a hug. "I'm so sorry for your worry. She's a fighter and right now is fairly stable. She will be having another kidney dialysis treatment momentarily, which assists her weakened kidneys to eliminate toxins that build up in her body. She has seemed to improve greatly now that this treatment was instituted yesterday." Sarah kept an eye on her vital signs on the bedside monitor even while talking to Caitlyn's parents.

Reine Sarantino rushed to her daughter's side, tears streaming down her face. "Caitlyn, my baby. I'm here. Mom is here." She thought back to the time she was pregnant with Caitlyn and how she resented the fact that she would have a child to interfere with her lifestyle. She employed nannies Caitlyn's whole life to care for her, giving her the freedom she demanded. She made sure no other child would be brought into the world to complicate her life even more. It was not until Caitlyn became an international star that she formed a bond with her.

Caitlyn stirred, struggling again just to open her eyes. She was conscious, but just so weak. She could think now. *What is wrong with my eyes? Just open, damn it! Why is my mom crying? I can hear her sniffling. I'm not dying. Just need some adjusting. Need my clone, damn it. Get that bitch!* With that, her eyes popped open. Reine surrounded her with her arms, kissing her cheeks and forehead.

"Mom," a raspy voice emerged.

"Yes, baby. Dad and I are here."

"Hi, sweetheart," came a voice from behind Reine. "What are you doing scaring us like this?"

"I'm sorry," she managed to say.

"Honey, don't be sorry. Just get well," her dad replied with his heart aching for his poor, desperately ill daughter.

Her color was not good. Her lips were purplish and face very pale. And those sunken eyes. He was so shocked by her features that he was near tears himself.

"Dad, you must find her," pleaded Caitlyn in a very weak voice.

"Find who, sweetheart?" He was puzzled at her request. Was she delirious or dreaming? What was she talking about?

Dr. Conrad cleared his throat. He was mad at himself for having the conversation on his phone with Dr. Burns in front of Caitlyn. She had been more alert than he had even thought. "She is referring to a slight delay in finding her clone. This is not an unusual occurrence," he added. "They're not always available at a moments notice."

Dr. and Mrs. Sarintino stared at each other in horror, then at Dr. Conrad. "Well, is there a problem? I mean, they will find her soon, right?"

"Sure. I'm very sure they will be notifying us any time now that she is in the hospital awaiting the harvesting." Sure I'm sure, he thought to himself. In fact, he was not so sure things were okay. "Well, if you will excuse me. Sarah will call me if she needs me." He smiled at Sarah and she gave him a thumbs-up in agreement.

"We'll be fine, sir," she stated, confidently.

Caitlyn, still with her eyes open, did not feel confident. She just wanted her clone found. Now. This missing clone belonged to her, and they needed to get her where she belonged.

Sarah could see her increasing anxiety through her vital signs. Her pulse was starting to race and her blood pressure was increasing. "Caitlyn, you must calm down. I'm going to give you a little relaxant to help you."

"No," Caitlyn was screaming inside. She wanted to remain awake. She had to keep insisting that everyone find this clone.

As she was drifting off, the last thing she heard was her mom saying, "Caitlyn, baby. We will fight for you. We'll find her. You just rest. We'll find her." As the medicine coursed through her veins, Caitlyn relaxed into a sound sleep.

"Reine," said Dr. Sarantino, "I have to find out how long a delay we are looking at." You stay with Cait and I'll find out what is going on."

CHAPTER 23

"Claire, what could have possibly happened to those three?" Barron asked as he paced the kitchen.

"I just can't even think that something awful happened," Claire said as she poured Barron a cup of coffee so he would sit down and stop pacing. "I know the road can be treacherous this time of year, but they have found no trace of any car off the road. They're searching with helicopters, horses and on foot. It's just unbelievable they have not been located."

"And what about their imbedded tracking system? Why on earth would that not be working?" Barron asked, just incredulous that this was happening.

"It's all just so confusing. I just want my girls to come home." Claire was almost to her breaking point. It had been twenty-four hours since the call from their community representative, Van, requesting that organs be harvested from Peyton. It was unexpected, certainly, as Peyton's OH would only be twenty-eight years old. What could possibly have happened to that young girl to need organ replacements already, thought Claire. She looked down and realized she was wringing her hands. She had never experienced this kind of fear -fear for her girls; the babies she had raised and the women she now was so proud of.

Barron got up and wrapped his arms around Claire. "I'm sure there is an explanation. I just know in my gut they are okay."

Claire asked, "Do you think the humans will enter our community to assist in the hunt?"

"Nope, never. They must rely on our people to hunt and find them. They can never enter for that reason. In fact, it was a pretty unusual circumstance to have the human dignitaries here. They are the only ones in the history of clone communities to ever set foot in one."

"Guess they are petty important guys."

"Yup," Barron said as he stared vacantly at the clock on the kitchen wall. "They had top-security secret service agents with them, too, at their first formal visit."

"They seemed to be pretty casual when they came back a couple days ago. I didn't see a big deal contingent of secret service with them. So couldn't they come back to join or head up the search?" asked a weary Claire. "Or bring in more help?"

"No human search party would be allowed without President Tavares or Dr. Christianson's authorization. And they would, indeed, have to accompany them. I'm sure they've been notified. They must be devastated with this news as you could tell they all were very fond of our girls."

"That's for sure. They seemed to have bonded and made a great team for the future of clones."

"Well, let's not lose our optimism." Barron guided Claire to a chair at the kitchen table. "I am going to fix you a warm cup of herbal tea and some flax chips. You have to try not to worry." He poured the cup with steaming water, which was always available from their wall spigot. "Our little ones will be coming home soon, and our baby will be waking up. We have to keep a brave face and not let them see our distress."

Claire slumped in her chair hoping she would be able to hide the despair she was feeling. "I will try, Barron."

Teams had been organized in all corners of the community. The supposed route was being tracked, and records perused to see what vehicle they used. All video camera tapes were now being reviewed. Computers sorted out the information at lightning speed. There was no doubt that the mystery of the girl's disappearance would be solved soon. It had to be.

CHAPTER 24

It was 8:00 pm, Swedish time and pitch dark as they neared their destination. Kirt had the airport in his instruments and was making a slow descent. The tower at the Swedish airport came on over the radio to confirm their approach and subsequent landing. Andre had tweaked the instrumentation to give a fictitious tail number, so they appeared to be ordinary tourists that frequented the area. The journey was arduous, flying zigzag over the Arctic Circle, to avoid any possible tracing of the flight.

"Andre," asked Kirt, now glad to have reached their destination. "Remember flying in here with dignitaries wanting to see the Ice Hotel?"

"Oh yeah" Andre grimaced and gave a shiver. "That's the last place I would want to see." Just then, Andre put the wheels down in preparation for landing. He and Kirt became very busy pushing buttons here and there and watching all their gauges to facilitate a perfect smooth landing.

Peyton, London and Abby awoke from their naps. "Wow," Peyton said as she stretched, yawned and squinted her eyes, not really ready to wake up. The cabin was fairly dark in preparation for the landing. "I guess all the excitement wore me out. "

Abby yawned following suit and said, "Time for a pit stop to freshen up."

"Ah, not now sweetie," said Johann laughing. "The wheels are down and we will be on the ground in less than two minutes."

"Darn. I must look dreadful," complained Abby.

"Are you kidding?" asked Miguel. "You still look stunning, muy bonita. I enjoyed watching you sleep."

"Nooo," screeched Abby as she blushed and hid her face beneath her creamy-brown, cardigan sweater. Her hair was now in two braids that Peyton had done to her, combating her boredom on the long flight. "You were watching me?" she continued to protest. "Did I snore or drool for you?"

Miguel let out a howl. "You are so funny, Abby and so, how do Americans say, fussy."

Peyton added to the laughter. "Well, I talk in my sleep so hope I didn't let out any top secrets."

"Hmmm," Miguel teased. "You did say something about Johann."

Peyton snapped her head toward Johann. "Shut up! Did I, Johann?"

Johann grinned. "Peyton, he's teasing you. I would not be disappointed if you had: as long as you said you adored me, of course, and not that you'd wish I'd get lost."

Peyton's face broke into a smile. "You know I wouldn't tell you to go away." She didn't know what was happening to her. The feelings she had for Johann were overwhelming. She just wanted to collapse in his arms, have him envelope her and yes, kiss her forehead as he had done before.

As they touched down, there was hardly any light coming through the windows. "Well, I guess we are not in Gay Parie, eh?" said Peyton with a disappointed sigh.

"Hardly," Johann replied. "But we are going to have a lot of fun holed up in a very quaint SWEDISH abode. You are going to learn lots of board games."

"We're in Sweden?" they all asked. "Not sure this would have been my pick over some fabulous, warm, tropical island," Abby said scowling. Somehow they had failed to learn of their destination when the plans were being implemented. Too late to protest.

"Whoopie," Peyton cheered sarcastically.

"You could take this time to learn to speak Swedish," said Johann.

"Swell." Peyton gave a mock smile.

"I can't wait," London broke in. "Just hope they have plenty of wine. What a vacation!"

"I already speak Swedish," added Abby as she peered out her window, trying to make out the terrain. "Just too dark," she whined.

"So do I," said Johann. "I'm half Swedish, if you three didn't know."

"Your name could have given them a clue, Joey," yelled back Kirt, who had been listening to this conversation as he guided the plane around the airport taxiway.

The girls laughed as Johann told them to stop in Swedish.

"I need to learn Swedish too, so you and Abby can't talk about me," piped in Miguel.

"I think you're going to be busy running the world, buddy," said Johann. "We'll be thinking of you while we're lounging around and you're at the world summit this week."

Just then the aircraft came to a stop. Kirt pulled himself out of his seat and came back to the cabin. "Okay, guys. In all seriousness, this is what we need to do. We are tourists coming to see the sights. No talking. Just act tired like you just woke up, and you don't want to be bothered." He pulled out a leather attaché and opened it. "Here are your fake IDs and passports. Miguel, you included. Once we are settled into our home, I will have a supper sent over. I have my cousins alerted, and they will be living with you to provide all necessities as well as protection."

"Your cousins?" asked Peyton warily.

"Hey, wait till you see them. No one messes with them. They are huge and well known around here. I know we're German, but they and I spent more time here in Sweden than in Germany. That's how I got to know Joey here. We've been pals since, what, five years old, Joey?"

"Something like that." Johann smiled, remembering all the good times they had in Sweden. "I don't remember spending much time in this, as you put it, quaint region, though. We're up at the tip and I'm already cold as hell." He pulled his sweatshirt hood over his head as he slipped on his parka.

We actually lived in Lulea, which is further down the coast and right on the water," explained Kirt, "but the weather was the same as here, you twit. You are just getting too sissified living in New York City with more mild winter temperatures."

Andre was already out the door talking in Swedish to two very large gentlemen.

"Hey, there are a couple of my cousins now." Remember, there are other people roaming around, so not a peep."

"Okeydokey." Peyton, London and Abby promised and ran their

fingers across their lips simultaneously like they were zipping their lips closed. They put on their enormous down-filled parkas with hoods that pretty much hid their faces. They already had put on thick, warm, wool pants, socks and thermal boots that went halfway up to their knees.

"Man, there is no way to be cold in these things," quipped Abby before they descended the plane's stairs. Each was clutching her passport in the event they were asked to show them. A dark car, the size of a stretch SUV, suddenly appeared and they were ushered into the back seat, followed by Miguel and Johann. Kirt and Andre were busy emptying and securing the airplane.

"I'll meet up with you later, guys," Kirt said as he put the last of the luggage and equipment into the rear of the SUV. "Andre and I need to take care of paperwork here," he said, busily writing on a clipboard. "We'll take care of customs. They know us and will assume, as usual that we're bringing some celebrities who don't want to be seen."

Miguel nodded and the two cousins hopped into the front and prepared to whisk them away. Kirt leaned in and said to Miguel. "We'll be taking off early tomorrow. No one will even know we made a detour on your way to France for your world summit."

"Ay, amigo. I'm sure there will be some scuttlebutt about a hiccup in the transplant system in the USA by the time I show up."

"Oh boy," Peyton exclaimed. "An adventure in the making."

Johann nodded in agreement. "Yeah, for all of us."

CHAPTER 25

"Barron, where could they be?" Claire asked frantically. Suddenly the phone rang. Claire rushed to answer it. "Hello? Have you found them? Nowhere in the community? How could they possibly have left without being seen by the cameras on all the borders? There's no way a car could have passed through undetected."

Barron spoke up. "I think we need to personally contact Johann and Miguel. Maybe they could help."

Claire was still listening on the phone. She put her hand over the mouthpiece and faced Barron with a frown. "Barron, they are telling me that Miguel is on his way to France for a world summit and Johann is tied up somewhere and out of touch right now." Tears were now streaming down her face.

"Claire, they will find them. I just know they are okay. They are survivors," he assured her.

Claire continued her conversation, "I will... I will let you know if I hear from either of them." She hung up the phone and collapsed into Barron's outstretched arms, unable to control her sobs.

Barron said, "I just hope the human military doesn't descend on us. It's illegal."

In between sobs Claire said, "You're sure they can't do anything here except on orders from President Miguel Tavares, right? They said they were going to search the perimeter on their side for any clues. Barron, I think the girls are really gone. But why?" Totally mystified, she just could not believe Peyton, of all people, would up and leave.

"I don't know," said Barron, "and it was her first chance to donate to her OH. It's the biggest gift and something we all are elated to do. The first time is especially rewarding. I just don't get..."

"Wait," screamed Claire. "That's it. Why would she disappear now? At this time? That has to be it, Barron. For some reason she does not want to donate."

Barron was incredulous. "How could that possibly be? She didn't even know, did she? She never said anything to us. But knowing Peyton, she must have had a reason. Oh, our poor, poor baby."

Suddenly there was a knock on the door. Barron hurried to open it to find their chief of security standing there, not looking very hopeful.

"Carl, please come in," said Barron as he shook his hand. "Claire, get some coffee for our friend." Carl removed his boots and laid his hat on the hallway table. "Let me take your coat," Barron said as he reached to help him slide out of the heavy parka.

"Barron, we have scoured the community. They are not here."

"You look exhausted, Carl," Claire said as she poured a steaming cup of coffee and handed it to him.

"Thanks, Claire. I appreciate your kindness." He gulped it, hoping it would renew his spirits as well as his energy. "I have to call the hospital and tell them our donor is going to be a no-show. We've done all we can to try to locate her."

"Carl, I think they flew out," Claire stammered with tears welling in her eyes again.

"What?" he sputtered as he was swallowing another gulp. "How could that have happened? No one has seen them anywhere around the airport. Not one camera has them even traveling anywhere. At least no car computer has tracked them. It's a mystery."

Barron broke in, "What about their microchip GPS? Any luck with that?"

"Nope, nothing. It's like they disappeared off the face of the earth. Somehow their chips have been turned off or are malfunctioning. It's just dumbfounding. It doesn't make sense." At this point he put his head in his hands, resting his elbows on the table in total defeat.

"She's gone for a reason, Carl. I know Peyton. She has a good reason, I am sure of it. And her sister, Abby, would back her all the way. London too."

"Well, all I know is we've done all we can. I hope her OH can find a substitute human donor. But nowadays they are hard to come by. And regenerating her own would just take too long."

"It is my understanding," Barron said as he got his own cup of coffee and plopped down next to Carl, "that this OH has very little time. She is pretty sick. Her poor parents must be devastated. Do you know who she is, Carl?" asked Barron.

"Well, we're not supposed to know, as you well understand, but it's all over the Internet. She's a very popular international figure."

"Yikes. I just don't understand," sighed Claire.

"I've heard that they will contact President Tavares tomorrow in France. He will probably institute a worldwide search for her. It's not just that she is clone to a very important person, but that protocol has been breached, and that's a serious matter," said Carl.

"Gosh, Carl. What will they do to her when they find her?" asked Claire.

"Don't know. This has never happened before. I'm sure some court has authority to rule on it, though."

Carl got up, going to the hall to retrieve his boots, coat and hat. As he was putting them on, he said, "So just sit tight. Nothing you or I can do about it."

"I'm still going to text her frequently just in case she can receive it. She's got to know we are desperate to find her and know she is safe." Claire had her cell phone clutched to her chest.

Carl looked at her with pity. "I suppose you can try, but I suspect that that has already been done," his voice skeptical.

"Carl, thanks for coming by." Barron walked to the door with him, one hand on his shoulder. "We sure do appreciate all that you are doing. Let us know the second you find out anything."

"I promise. You too," he replied as he headed toward his car.

Claire and Barron just stood there, both still in disbelief of the uncertainty of the last two days.

"Claire, let's bundle up the kids and go out for a stroll. We can't do anything just sitting around and we need a fresh perspective on this." Barron was trying to comfort Claire as he forced an unconvincing smile.

She nodded. "Yes, our poor kids have been feeling the effects of our worry and we should spend some time with them."

One tear made its way down her cheek. Barron brushed it aside with his warm hand. He kissed her gently, feeling the pain she was in. Even clones had tender, caring feelings.

CHAPTER 26

Kirt's cousins may have been big and scary-looking, but their other side sure was astonishing. Who knew? They could cook. And what a breakfast feast lay before them.

Peyton sauntered out of the bedroom, prompted by the wonderful smells of rich coffee and pastries, fresh from the oven. It was only 5:00 am in New York, but already 11:00 am here. They had anticipated they would have jet lag. But since they flaked out last night at midnight Swedish time, 7:00 pm New York time, they had gotten plenty of sleep. They had even napped on the plane. Peyton could not remember the last time she had slept so long. The events of the last twenty-four hours had taken its toll on her. Andre and Kirt thrived on no sleep. They and Miguel had been up and out of the house hours ago.

Abby finally stumbled in like it was the middle of the night. It was hard to tell what time it was due to the winter season and no sunshine. "What time is it, and for that matter, what day is it? I am so disoriented," she spouted as she reached over the counter for a cup of coffee. Normally she would not indulge in caffeine, but she begged for it now. "Give me that human brew," she demanded. Her normally large, bright, blue eyes were now at half-mast. Her long blond locks were tossed all over her head.

"Where's our London?" asked Peyton, who also was dragging. Her hair was carelessly pulled back into a scrunchy, odds and ends of locks peeking out and falling around her face. Her natural beauty, even after just crawling out of bed and with no makeup on, was extraordinary. "Is she already up and out exploring ahead of us?"

"That she is," spoke up Kirt's cousin, Heinz. But we sent Hilka with her so she stays out of trouble," he smiled. "We let you go too, after you eat, eh?"

"Good deal. But I'm starved and it smells so wonderful. Now you know we are vegetarians, right?" asked Peyton.

"Nein. You scrawny frauleins need fattening up so we turn you into Viking women."

Ahhh, I don't think so," Abby said, looking nervous and glancing at Peyton.

Peyton started laughing hysterically. "Abby, he's putting you on. You are, right? Heinz?" Now Peyton was scowling at him and pleading for an answer.

"OK, you win. The meal is as you wish. We have frauleins that also are vegan, so they have prepared us for your special meal choices. They are actually here with us to make sure we do it right," he admitted.

Peyton and Abby let out squeals of relief. Beef or chicken had never touched their lips and they weren't about to try it now.

They dug into the delicious breakfast set before them and loved every bite of omelet with sausage and gravy, and none of it with animal products.

"Yum," said Peyton. "This sausage and gravy is great. I need to take you guys back with us to New York. She was careful not to say the "community" as she was not sure how much they knew. She assumed the cousins would think they were totally human.

Abby was chowing down, not even caring about being lady-like. "You definitely need to return with us. Wouldn't Claire and Barron love to copy these recipes?" As she said it, her heart suddenly ached. "Oh my gosh. Our poor family must be frantic over our sudden disappearance. I wish we could contact them just to let them know we are alive and well." She looked over at Peyton who now was twirling her fork around her plate, eyes downcast.

"Abs, we can't. Not yet. They are strong and you know they have lots of faith in us. In their heart they know we are fine."

She quickly changed the subject. "So what's on the agenda? Has Miguel left yet?" asked Abby.

Long gone," said Peyton. "Off to Parie."

"Darn. I didn't even get to say adios."

"He'll be back soon," came a voice from the doorway.

"Johann, you're up?" asked Peyton.

"Yeah, you slackers. I've been up for hours, working. I have my computer set up in the den, outfitted with a scrambler, of course. People still think I'm holed up in my New York apartment." He gave a shrug with a smirk on his face. He walked over to the counter to get another cup of coffee. Abby and Peyton giggled.

"OK, so are you used to your new names? Start using them with each other so you're not caught off guard," he demanded. "Keep your altered IDs on you too when you go out."

He was very concerned about keeping hidden and really did not even want anyone going out, but knew that would be difficult with these girls. "You can go out with Heinz or Hilka, but please stay quiet. No chitchatting. Most of the time, expect to stay here. Less chance of being spotted. Remember, today all hell is going to break loose. Miguel is going to have to give an order for a worldwide search for Peyton."

"I'm so scared, Johann," Peyton said as she started to tremble. Her heart was thundering in her chest. "What's going to happen to you if they find me?"

"I don't care about myself. I'm so worried about you."

"What a mess I've put you in," she said, tears streaming down her face.

"Peyton, I've chosen to be in this mess. I thought we already had this conversation. I care about you, and I'm not going to let them touch you." He crossed the room and took her into his arms. Peyton melted into him. He kissed her head, taking in the fragrant scent of her shiny, disheveled hair. He brushed a fallen strand out of her face and kissed her on her nose. Peyton felt warm, protected and content like she had never felt before meeting this human. If this was what humans referred to as love, then she was in love-totally.

Abby near tears said, " You two are unbelievable. We are from two different worlds. How can you combine them? What are you two going to do about this?"

Johann spoke very quietly. "I don't have an answer for you, Abby. But I do know, I'm not letting Peyton go. Whether I live in your world or she in mine, I will never let her go."

Peyton's quiet sobs were stifled by burying her face into Johann's chest. She was holding onto him like her life depended on it. And in reality, it did.

"Breakfast over," Heinz said as apparently no one was eating at this point. "Board game time," he announced.

Peyton peeked out from under Johann's arms, wiped her tears and started to smile. "Thanks, Heinz. I need to chill out."

Suddenly the door flung open and in bounced effervescent London. "Hey sleepyheads, about time you got up." She threw off her voluminous parka, hat with wide brim, dark glasses and boots.

"Talk about camouflage, London," said Abby.

"Yeah, pretty good, huh? The only thing showing was my chin and tip of my nose. Don't think anyone could recognize me. If anyone asked me anything, I acted dumb, like I am anyway. Nothing new there," she chuckled.

"Alright, already!" shouted Heinz. "You like my American slang? Learned that from Kirt. Let's get to it, eh?

"Count me out, Heinz," Johann called back as he walked toward the den. Wish I could play, but work beckons me. Kirt, my boss man, will call me on the carpet if I don't get some work done today. I'll join you later," he said with a wave of his hand.

Peyton watched him return to the den. She enjoyed the rear view as much as the front. Those adorable buns and neck-length hair, uncombed and wild, going every which way at the moment, totally captivated her. She wanted so much to go in, keep silent and just watch him work. But instinct told her she would be a distraction. And she would be right.

The girls and Heinz, along with his cousin Fritz, sat down for what would be hours of hilarity, yelling and typical board-game antics.

CHAPTER 27

"I can't believe we've been here one whole week," said Peyton, passing a steaming plate of breaded eggplant with garlic pasta to Johann.

"I know you must be getting cabin fever, Peyton, but I personally have been enjoying the meals. Yum. A little bit of Swedish, a little bit of German, and all vegetarian cuisine. And working from my computer with no politicians interrupting me is delightful. I really could stay for a month or two. All I need is my computer. I see them and they see me. It is totally like being there but without the hassle. No late-night dinners with diplomats."

"But what about all the meetings and community visits that are on your agenda? How much longer can you give excuses for not being present?" Peyton was sipping a glass of wine and totally enjoying the exceptional pasta.

"Oh, that's easy. Ask Kirt. He is a master of finding excuses for my not showing up." His boyish grin made Peyton burst out in laughter.

"I'm sure you two make quite a team," she giggled.

"But don't forget, he's also is a tough taskmaster, so I don't get away with it too often," he countered. "Pass me some more pasta please. Without Kirt looking over my shoulder, I can take seconds."

Abby spoke up between bites. "We need to get back to our five-mile runs, sister, or in another week we won't be fitting into the jet seats to fly back home. You too, Johann, you pasta hound."

"Speaking of which," said Peyton. "What's going on in the human world?"

"I spoke with Miguel just before dinner. They have instituted a worldwide search. Your picture is everywhere."

"What? How can that be?" Peyton dropped her fork and looked in disbelief at Johann. "No one has my picture. No one has ever seen me."

"Peyton," Johann said, looking into her wide, frightened eyes. "You look exactly like your OH. They just took her picture and posted it. They gave several versions with brown, blond and blondish-red hair. They don't need your actual picture. You and your OH are extraordinarily beautiful. No one could mistake you."

"Oh man," she signed.

"That's why I really don't want you going out. If you have to, you must wear a hat, sunglasses and lots of clothes to try to look fat," he laughed.

"So," Abby spoke up again. Wine glass in hand, she gestured, almost spilling the German Riesling. "What are they doing to look for us?"

"Well to start with, broadcasting the story on every TV station in the world. There are CIA and Secret Service agents along with military on alert. All of this just for some spoiled, superstar, daddy's girl." Johann visibly became more and more irritated. He grabbed his wine and downed the entire glass in one gulp.

Peyton stared at him as she saw how upset he had become. "What are you talking about? Is that what they're saying about her?"

Just then Kirt and Andre came bursting through the kitchen side door.

"Hello, gang!" yelled Kirt.

"Hey, you're back," the girls shouted back. "How was Paris? Did you stop over to Germany to see your family? How is Miguel? When is he coming back?" They were pummeling him with questions nonstop.

"Whoa," he responded as he greeted each one with a hug. "Let me get me some hot food before I handle all your questions." He grabbed a warm bun and picked up Abby's knife and spread butter on it before downing it in three bites. "I am famished. Come on, Andre. Grab some plates and I'll get the silverware," as he scurried around the kitchen. Heinz brought out more sauce and pasta, piping hot.

Johann watched the girls squirming and pestering Kirt until Kirt finally answered between swallows.

"Fine, yes, fine and I don't know." He winked at Johann.

"Ah, my man," Johann finally got a word in edgewise. "It's good to see you. I've been a good boy and have been working diligently." He actually had been busy taking care of all his tasks.

"So I have witnessed," he agreed. I've stayed up with you by snooping on your computer from afar."

"Yeah, that and your calls five times a day," he reminded him.

"Uh, yup," as he went back to eating in silence, enjoying the meal.

Now it was Johann's turn to ask questions. "What's the latest today?"

"The CIA is baffled. They, so far, have no clue. But that said, they have surmised that the only way out of Community 27 had to be by air. They are going to figure it out soon, I'm afraid. I may have to join you living incognito. If they link Miguel, then we are in double trouble. Really big trouble." He picked up his wine glass and toasted everyone with, "One for all and all for one."

Johann asked, "What is the situation with Caitlyn? I have been so busy with my projects that I have not been in the loop. And I haven't asked. I don't want to appear at all interested."

"It is not good for her. She is gravely ill. I don't think she can last much longer. There are no other options for her either."

"Well, all I can hope is that we're not found. And this is over in short order."

"Time to lighten this dirge," announced Heinz as he came in with a tray of ice cream parfaits and a side tray of hot fudge and whipped cream.

Peyton, Abby and London all screamed. "We hate you! You know that will immediately go from our lips to our hips in nanoseconds."

"Besides," said Abby, "we don't eat dairy, so we are saved. Phew!"

"Not to fear, my tiny earthlings. This is frozen soy dessert and no added sugar at that."

"Bring it on!" they howled.

"Well it does still have calories," insisted Peyton, "but who cares. We need comfort food."

"I'll run with you tomorrow," promised Johann. "But it has to be at 5:00 am before anyone awakens. It will be nippy too."

"I don't think nippy is quite the word I would use," Peyton said as she wrapped her arms around herself. "It's darn cold. I have never experienced such bone-chilling temperatures in my life. But I don't care. We have to do it. I have to stay in my routine."

Just then the phone rang. It was Miguel. Johann put it on speaker. "Those damn US CIA guys are too good," he announced.

"What's going on Miguel?" Johann inquired as he glanced nervously at Kirt.

"They figured out the girls had to have left by air. There couldn't be any other explanation. They have linked Kirt's flying in and out at about that time, although they have no idea where he went as there was no record due to Kirt's expert scrambling of the aeronautics."

"Thank God for our ability to do that," muttered Kirt.

"Have they suspected either of us being involved?" asked Johann.

"Don't think so. They have not figured out that I came to France on Kirt's plane, but someone did spot Kirt in Germany, so they knew he was on this continent. Also, I hope you're sitting down. The latest is they somehow have your plane landing in Sweden."

"Okay. Crap," Kirt said. "So they confiscate my plane…"

Before he could finish, Heinz, who just hung up his cell phone, interrupted. "My cousins saw the Feds nosing around the plane and when they weren't looking, they took off with it. Smart guys that they are, they get it from me," he added smugly. The aeronautics is still scrambled so there is no clue to its destination. They will let us know where they end up."

"Hey, compradres," Miguel piped in, "you got to get out of there. And I mean this second. Every country has their most astute investigators hunting you, and I'm afraid they are on your trail. You are in immediate danger."

They all looked at each other in horror.

Heinz said, "I'm on it, Miguel. My guys are already on their way and should be here within minutes, and we will smuggle them to another place somewhere."

"Thanks, Heinz. I knew I could count on you and know you will do your best."

Johann said, "Miguel, are you safe? Are you sure they haven't tied you in yet?"

"Nope, not yet. So far, Community 27 has not offered them the info that you or I were there."

Peyton looked at Johann with a questioning look. "I have the feeling Barron and Claire have figured it out by now and are keeping quiet. I know they must think there is a logical reason for my sudden disappearance and don't want to tip their hand. They have great intuition."

"Go now. Don't waste time," Miguel yelled. "Call me when you are safe, guys." With that he hung up.

Heinz and the women scrambled to get food and water tossed into a duffle bag. They threw on their warmest parkas and wool socks and pants, and finally their knee-high thermal boots. They also put on wool hats under the parka hoods and double gloves. They were prepared for whatever cold encounter they may face.

A dark, oversized SUV with tinted windows pulled up to the front of the house. The equipment was snatched up and thrown into duffle bags, which were thrown over their backs and hauled to the waiting vehicle. They all jumped in and within seconds, the SUV roared away, leaving only one female cousin to act as a decoy. She had no fear to do this as she was actually trained in espionage and was savvy when it came to Secret Service tactics.

It was not five minutes before three black cars, also with dark, tinted windows, pulled up to the house. Out jumped multiple identically dressed men with black wool coats and wool caps with earpieces fitting down over their ears. Three or four secured the perimeter of the house while four others knocked on the door.

Enga opened the door with a calm smile and welcomed them in. "Can I help you gentlemen?" she asked in Swedish.

"We have information that would lead us to believe there are Americans here," said the one with the dark, menacing eyes, which were darting around the room.

"We many times have American tourists," she said. "They come to see the Ice Hotel and enjoy our wonderful culture as well as…"

He abruptly cut her short. He signaled with his black-gloved hand to the other men to spread out and search the place.

"Excuse me, sir," said Enga, emphatically, but sweetly. "Did you ask me if you could barge into my home? Do you have a search warrant? We may be pretty far north, but we do have laws, you know." She now was starting to show her anger, playing it up well.

The dark one glared at her and said, "It is a secret service thing and you don't need to see a search warrant."

"Once again, excuse me," she protested. "I don't care what you call it. Get out of my inn."

The other three thugs were finished looking anyway and threw up their arms and shrugged. "Nothing here, Chief."

He turned on his heels and said over his shoulder, "We are not done here. We will be back with a team to go over your inn with a fine-tooth comb. I can assure you of that. And with all the legal documentation."

With that, they all left and hopped back into their cars and took off.

Enga made one call. "Now," she said.

Within five minutes, ten women descended on the house, coming from nearby homes. With them came vacuum cleaners, cleaning supplies, mops and buckets. Every single thing was scrubbed, vacuumed, and all traces of evidence quickly eliminated. Not as much as one stand of hair or fingerprint remained. Once done, they all left, including Enga.

CHAPTER 28

Heinz knew all the back roads and expertly traversed the small town. They were on a deserted highway within minutes. "I did not want to resort to this," Heinz told them, "but it now appears we have no other choice."

Johann was grinning with his deep, blue eyes now looking ever more mischievous.

The girls looked at each other, then back at Johann. They had no clue what this zany bunch was up to. They looked at Kirt for an explanation. He joined the guys with a knowing smile.

"Alright," pleaded Abby. "What in the name of heaven are you up to? We are scared here and you're acting like this is some kind of game." She was clutching Peyton, who usually was more of a baby than she.

"You know, Abby," said Peyton, "I don't know why, but somehow I feel safe with these crazy, lunatic guys."

Johann reached over and took Peyton's hand. He then reached over and patted Abby on the shoulder. The unflappable, optimistic London was cuddled up to Kirt and had not a care in the world. "We are going to our favorite hiding place," explained Johann. No one knows about it except all us buddies. It was a favorite place to hide out when we were young and occasionally, now and then, when the world gets a little crazy and we need a break."

Heinz piped in, "I hope you gals don't get seasick, as we have to take a little boat ride."

"Oh my gosh," shrieked Abby. "And how would we know about being seasick? Do you think we have an ocean in New York State?" They all roared.

"Well Abby, I couldn't care less how sick it may make us," Peyton said. "We are escaping." Peyton glared at her with sisterly scorn. Then she turned to Johann with questioning eyes. "Ahaaa, and where are we escaping to?"

Kirt said, "That's the fun part. We have a secret cave on a deserted island…uh, well not exactly an island, but a piece of land, uh well, sorta a piece of rock in the Barents Sea."

"Are you guys totally out of your mind?" Abby became slightly freaked out at this point.

The boys were still smiling, knowing how they were terrifying the girls. "Okay, let's stop scaring them." Johann turned to look straight at the girls. "Actually, over the years we have put in creature comforts. Maybe not fancy as you had in New York, but still it it's not a bat cave."

Kirt said, "Yeah, I insisted on heat. We have a solar generator for electricity, lights and heat pump. We used to have just a fire pit, piping the smoke out the top, and we had to use down sleeping bags. Now that was fun. We still use the fire pit to grill steaks."

The girls shuddered at the thought. Their first concern was how one would take a bath. "Wouldn't someone see the smoke?" asked London.

Heinz added, "It's not in a shipping lane so is virtually isolated and unknown. We happened to stumble upon it when sailing these waters as young lads. We liked to push the envelope and venture into uncharted territory to see if we could survive and make our way back. We had such an unadulterated sense of adventure back then. Young and probably pretty foolish. But look at us. It made us the rugged, charming men that we are."

Kirt added, "We were hoping we would not have to go to this extreme to hide you, but if we must, we must." The guys then again broke into laughter.

"What is up with you insane people?" asked Abby, still trying to comprehend everything.

"You don't understand, Abby," Kirt said. "We love it there. It is our man cave."

"Literally," added Johann, as he couldn't stop laughing.

Kirt continued. "We were not ever going to share its existence with anyone, ever, but now we have to and are okay with that as we know it's our only chance not to be found. Truly, you will be safe."

"Yeah, if we survive the confinement," said Abby, looking doubtful.

"Abby, trust me," Johann said. "It has a large-screen TV, computers, all kinds of computer games, pool tables…"

"Okay. We get it," said Peyton. "So we are going to your utopia."

"I guess you could say that. We just didn't think you would be happy in a cave, so we didn't go there in the first place. But now it's necessary. And yeah, we're not that disappointed that we're ending up there." That wide grin returned.

Peyton sighed at Johann. A smile started forming across her face in spite of her doubts about this place. Johann just melted her with his eyes and she did trust his judgment. Suddenly, another question came to her, "What about food and…" She did not even finish her question when Heinz interrupted.

"Believe it, Peyton, it's stocked. And your cook is right here," as he pointed to himself.

They finally relaxed and trusted that they were in good hands.

The road was rough and it was getting very dark. Heinz and his cousins knew this road well so had no problem navigating it. They finally arrived at a seaport.

"We're here. We'll pull up to the yacht. You all be ready to board quickly. Have your face hidden in your parkas. We don't expect anyone around, but just in case," instructed Heinz. "Once you are out of the SUV with all the gear and equipment, I will take the car to our hidden hut. It's not far, so I'll sprint back."

The yacht was gigantic. The girls scrambled aboard across the gangplank and into a large, open room. Johann, Kirt and Andre followed with duffle bags loaded with their stuff. It was not long before Heinz joined them. Four other cousins were already on board. They had left well in advance of them, so had the yacht warmed up and ready to go. They pulled out of the bay within minutes of their arrival.

"You can relax for awhile," announced Johann. "The trip over is about two hours, and that's traveling at 150 to 200 mph. You won't feel anything as this yacht goes over the water, not in it; it's a hovercraft. Actually Heinz was kidding about seasickness. You'll just experience a lulling motion."

"Wait," yelped Peyton. "How can your cousins see where they are going at that speed? What if another boat is out there?" Her eyes were big as saucers and she had a definite panicked look on her face. At this point, Abby joined her.

"Man, how could two sisters who are not sisters be so much alike?" Johann was shaking his head and trying not to laugh. He knew they really were frightened and he should not tease them. "They have radar and autopilot, Peyton. The yacht will automatically avoid anything in its way. Not to worry, you two."

Peyton gave a big sigh as she finally took off her jacket, boots, gloves and hat. She was glad she had on a thick, warm turtleneck tonight. Who would have known she would be heading to a cave in the middle of a freezing ocean?

Johann started to laugh out of the blue. He was sitting back on a large, cushiony couch with his now bootless feet up on a coffee table in front of him. He patted the spot next to him, inviting Peyton to come sit down.

She obliged and plopped down, cuddling up to him. She immediately started to relax. "So what are you laughing about?" she demanded.

"Well, I was just thinking. No woman has ever set foot in our man cave. We made a pact as young studs that never, ever would we bring a chick to our man cave."

Kirt was joining them now. "Yeah, well Joey, we kept that promise as long as we could."

"Do you feel bad that we're ruining your pact?" asked Abby.

"Hell no," said Kirt. London then came over and playfully hit him on the side of his head. "London, what was that for?" he asked.

"You guys and your secrets. Is that a human thing? We would never do that, right girls? Our guys either."

"Uh, London, I don't think our guys are quite wired like these studs. They don't think of themselves either. They only think about taking care of their family and children and of the community and most importantly, of serving their OH."

"What the hell is an OH?" asked Heinz so totally in the dark about these clone things.

"It means original human, buddy. I will explain later. I guess you never heard the abbreviated term before."

"Guess I really never paid much attention. I've never needed my clone and actually had put it out of my mind."

Johann patted Peyton's knee and she sank down deeper into the couch, her legs curled up, her head on Johann's chest. She drifted off to sleep with the slight motion of the boat.

London and Kirt were talking and laughing, while Abby was alone in a recliner, missing Miguel. She sure hoped he had not been found out. Did he know about this place? Could he join them? She knew that would be impossible. She drifted off to sleep as well.

It was around midnight when the slowing of the engine woke up Peyton and Abby. Johann had laid Peyton across the couch once she was asleep. Abby slept comfortably in the recliner. Both were now stretching and yawning.

"Are we there yet?" asked Peyton, trying to see out of the windows.

"Yup, we're there," said Kirt. "We will slip into a bay, which is its own cave. It is not real easy to walk, so take care. You will be walking around a ledge to get to the man cave." Every time he said 'man cave', he chuckled.

They put on all their warm outer gear as it was no warmer here than in Sweden. Johann went out first and felt a blast of freezing air in his face. "Cover up good, gals. It's a mite chilly."

"Yeah, I bet a mite chilly," said Abby. She followed him with trepidation. The cold, salty air almost took her breath away. She immediately pulled her wool scarf up over her mouth and nose. "Where the hell are we? The frickin North Pole?"

"Almost," answered Kirt.

In just a matter of a few minutes, they had all managed to gingerly walk around the ledge without anyone falling into the water. It was deep and ominous, waves splashing against the walls of the cave. The water that managed to land on the ledge froze instantly and made for a very dangerous trek. Soon they were entering the front door. A front door, thought Peyton. She did not know what to expect, but a front door was not really what she had envisioned.

"A front door. Oh my goodness," cried out Peyton.

"What did you think?" asked Johann.

"I don't know. Usually caves just have, you know, openings, like holes."

"You are not in New York, my dear. This is not Howe's Cavern."

London, Peyton and Abby walked into a lighted room. Warm air, to their surprise, blasted them. It was an actual cozy home. "How on earth did you do this?" London asked in total wonder.

"It wasn't easy," Kirt said.

"Yeah, it took years of sneaking stuff over here without anyone getting suspicious," added Johann.

"I made tons of trips too," said Heinz. My cousins helped a lot. We pooled our talents to do electrical wiring and plumbing."

"That was going to be my next question," said London.

"Yes, we have indoor plumbing. Well, sort of, that is. The commode is inside, but is just a seat with a very long tunnel to the sea beneath."

"Sounds good to me. At least we don't have to trek to an outhouse." London gave a huge sigh of relief.

"Hey, creature comforts," Kirt added. "And the shower is heated."

"Ready for a tour?" Kirt motioned the gals to follow him. The girls stared at everything, incredulous of what they were seeing. Somehow the guys had built walls and ceilings within the cave. There were three bedrooms with two sets of bunk beds in each, a game room with TV, sofas, pool table, table and chairs presumably for playing board games, and a large open fireplace.

"Unbelievable," exclaimed Abby. "So you sneak off to this place to get away from the stress, eh?"

"You got it," Kirt said. "For almost ten years now."

So now we wait," Peyton said, matter-of-factly.

"I don't think it will be long, Peyton. Once the threat is gone...." meaning once her OH was dead, thought Peyton..."we'll come out of hiding to face the world and explain the facts." Johann was pretty convinced everything would turn out okay. "Not everyone will side with us, but I think most will."

"I hope you're right, Johann," said Peyton. "Otherwise your career is over, the clones will be in a compromised position and Miguel will likely face an impeachment if it's discovered he was an accessory."

"Let's not worry about any of that. The main thing is that you are safe and I care about you more than anything in the world. Peyton, I love you." Johann took her face in his hands and lovingly kissed her on her lips, long and passionately. She was swept away.

CHAPTER 29

Nurses bustled around to the sounds of hissing ventilators, beeping heart monitors and hushed tones of health care workers attending to the critical patients.

Dr. Conrad walked into unit 7, chart in hand. Lines across his forehead and his grimace pretty much told the story of his grave concern. "Sarah, how are the liver enzymes looking?"

Sarah looked up from administering medications into Caitlyn's central line port. "All her indices are heading south," she sighed with defeat in her voice. "She's shutting down. Her liver is now worsening and she continues in renal failure. Look at her heart rate." She pointed to the heart monitor. The bleeps were fast and erratic. "She's struggling."

Dr. Conrad let out an exasperated sigh. "Sarah, I don't think there is anything else we can do. It's too late now even if we did find her clone. Too many organs are failing simultaneously. I'm afraid we are just hours away from death. Too bad. She would have had a good chance of survival even twenty-four hours ago if we could have located her clone." He shrugged and stared at the young life that was about to end.

Sarah nodded. "It's too bad," she agreed. "Her parents are devastated and understandably furious about the failure to find her clone."

"Are they still here?"

"Yes, in the family suite waiting room."

"I will go speak to them." He took out his stethoscope and listened to Caitlyn's lungs just to verify that his conclusion was correct. "She's developed rales in her lungs, adding airway obstruction to our list. Sarah, when was the last time she was conscious?"

"Probably yesterday afternoon. She was still cursing and pleading for help."

"Poor thing. She may rally again, but I suspect it won't be long before her organs will no longer be viable to sustain her. Guess I better go and talk to the Sarantinos. They need to know the gravity of the situation."

"I think they know in their minds what the probable outcome is for Caitlyn. But in their hearts…they are not going to be ready for this. Good luck."

The room was dimly lit, walls a soft pastel, adorned with serene paintings. The atmosphere offered families a sense of peace and hope. The scenes of sunsets, rainbows, beautiful mountains and streams were all displayed beautifully and accentuated by direct lighting. The room incorporated overstuffed chairs and couches expertly placed in groupings to accommodate several families simultaneously. Opening to the main room, a hallway led to four bedrooms. Off to the side was a well-equipped kitchen. Light streamed in from the picture windows, making it cheerful and inviting. There were several tables covered with teal and green-leaf tablecloths adding to the ambiance. The refrigerator, stocked with fresh fruits, vegetables and drinks, offered a wide variety of options. Worried, waiting family members could also order full meals from chefs in the hospital's main kitchen. There was an aide on duty twenty-four/seven to assist the families.

Dr. Conrad strode in, observing the amenities, and thought to himself, that this area is so helpful to stressed families who otherwise would be sitting in hallways or stark waiting rooms like in times past. But all this was not going to mean a hill of beans to Caitlyn's grief stricken parents. The Sarantinos are going to lose their baby girl, and it could have been prevented. If only we could have found her clone. Where the hell could she be? And why did she disappear? He could not hide the disappointment on his face. He spotted the Sarantinos sitting by the window, chatting quietly. Their faces looked distraught and weary; tears streamed down Reine's face. Her husband's eyes were red and vacant.

Dr. Conrad walked over and sat down in an adjacent chair. The sun shone in, belying the horrible dark cloud he was about to evoke. "I'm so sorry, Dr. Sarantino, Mrs. Sarantino. There is nothing more we can do."

"Could we not have gotten a human cadaver to replace her failing organs?" asked Dr. Sarantino, pleading for a remedy.

"I'm sorry. First, human cadavers are few and far between because humans use their clones to extend their lives. Even in the event a cadaver were available, not having been saved by its own clone, the likelihood of it having salvageable parts would be slim, and it most certainly would not have enough viable organs to give Caitlyn. She needed so many. Secondly, the rejection factor also would overwhelm her due to using an unrelated human donor for so many organs, even if they were available. I'm not sure she would have been able to tolerate so many antibodies invading her blood stream. Our only hope was to transplant from her clone."

Tears now flowed from both their eyes. There was no hope. They were going to lose Caitlyn. The world was going to lose Caitlyn, a beloved icon.

"May we go in now and be with her till the end?"

"Of course," Dr Conrad whispered, on the verge of tears himself.

They all stood up, Reine gripping her husband, wobbling with grief and sorrow. Dr. Conrad hugged them and escorted them down the short hall to the ICU.

CHAPTER 30

"Mr. President, we have just received word Ms. Caitlyn is not expected to survive much longer. In fact, we are anticipating her demise at any moment.

Miguel nodded to his secretary. After the door closed, he breathed a sigh of relief. One hurdle over, he said to himself. Now to figure out how to return Peyton to her community and explain to the world the necessity of hiding her. Caitlyn was such a well-loved celebrity. Would people side with her family and have preferred to sacrifice Peyton, a lowly clone, to save the life of Caitlyn? Miguel was not looking forward to the next chain of events. He pulled out his cell phone and dialed Kirt, knowing no one could unscramble his hi-tech communication device.

"Hey, capitan, mi amigo," answered Kirt. "How's everything shaking out?"

"Won't be long, jefe," he replied, with no emotion. Miguel gazed out his window, watching Parisians passing by, unaware of the tragic news that they would soon be hit with. Caitlyn was France's daughter, a part of their culture even. They had bragging rights with all her success. Sadly, with the spotlight on her tragic end, the real story of her wild, self-destructive life could permeate the media. Maybe the news outlets will be kind to her and be respectful and not reveal the tawdry side of her life.

"Miguel, you still there?" asked Kirt, as he was not sure if their communication had been cut.

"I'm here. Tell Johann to hang in there. I need to see how this is going to play out. We may need to wait long enough for the furor to die down before making an appearance."

"No hurry on this end," said Kirt, grinning. "The girls may be feeling a little homesick, missing their family, but we're certainly comfortable. We have enough rations to last us weeks if need be. Oh, and Miguel, a certain little blond fraulein misses you and is a tad worried."

"Is that right?" Miguel smiled broadly as he thought of Abby. "Assure her I am fine and this will be over soon. I'm plotting now about how and when we will present to the world. We will keep everyone safe, and hopefully, our careers will survive intact," he quipped with a nervous laugh.

Just then Johann grabbed the phone from Kirt. "Hey, mi amigo, any theories out there as to the clones' location? Have they concluded that I am connected to the disappearance? I surmise poor Kirt is already implicated."

Kirt bowed with one hand in back and one in front, facetiously proud of his astounding feat. Johann winked at him. Grinning at his antics, the girls surrounded Kirt and plastered him with hugs and kisses. Making light of a very serious situation helped them all to cope. In reality, he was in a very dangerous predicament.

"Kirt certainly is a very serious contender in their investigation and intense search. You, Joey, so far are not mentioned. Remember, they are not getting any help from Community 27. They know nothing and saw nothing. The only connection is Kirt's plane going in and out of Community 27. All logs were scrambled so they can't trace the plane, though. Remember, they also have evidence of a sighting of Kirt in Germany, and then Sweden before the plane vanished. By the way, Johann, where did that plane go? No one has seen it."

Johann glanced at Kirt. "Oh, Miguel, you know how Kirt's cousins are. They could have taken a joyride to some southern, remote island with it. And I mean remote."

"Ha haha," laughed Miguel. "What a team. You scoundrels are better than any top-secret-service agents of mine. Got to run. Will call you muchachos soon. It sounds like you guys are handling your boredom well."

"Boredom, my ass," snapped Johann. "I'm still working, well a little anyway. And the girls are mastering one game after another, killing us."

"Hasta luego," said Miguel.

"Yeah, later." Johann hung up and took a deep breath. He looked across the room and locked eyes with Peyton. He had never known this kind of love. This kind of unconditional devotion to this woman, his willingness to give up everything he had worked so hard for and putting his life on the line, were new to him. He knew, if found, he could be shot on sight. He smiled and winked at Peyton as she stood there with an inquisitive look on her face.

CHAPTER 31

They arrived from all over the world: Dignitaries, business giants and celebrities. The mood of the world was grim. Never in history had a clone not been available for its OH other than in a circumstance of premature death.

Johann would need to make an appearance, after all, it was a known fact he and Caitlyn had been an item, albeit briefly. The fact that he was in charge of clone communities, also made it imperative that he attend.

"Johann," said Peyton, "I'm so worried about your going back to New York. What if someone has figured out you were instrumental in my escape?"

"Peyton, I have to take that chance. They would be suspicious if I didn't surface." Johann drew her to him, enveloping her as she wept quietly. He kissed her passionately then stepped back to study her one last time. He looked over at Abby. "Abby, you two hang in there and take care of Peyton. I will call whenever I can." He hugged everyone, including Kirt, giving him manly pats on his back. He turned and walked to the front door, feeling the blast of arctic air as he opened it. He traversed the slippery ledge and made his way to the waiting boat.

The cousins would have a jet waiting at the port to usher him back to Teteboro. He would miss his constant companion, but knew it was too risky for Kirt to emerge. He probably was already being implicated. Johann would schedule some face-to-face meetings while in New York to indicate life as usual. He'd probably have to make a public statement once he was brought up to speed on the status of the investigation. He looked forward to seeing Miguel, who was due in for the funeral.

It was cold and blustery as the caisson made its way to St. Patrick's Cathedral. The streets were lined with mourners, undeterred.

Johann and Miguel sat in the front pew along with the family of Caitlyn. They exchanged knowing glances, begging for this torture to be over. Large overhead screens displayed Caitlyn's life throughout the years, and it appeared this tribute was going to last for hours. Johann squirmed in his seat just thinking about it. The church was packed to standing room only, and he knew personal testimonies alone could take an hour. Thank God he was not asked to give one, not that he would have agreed to.

Johann leaned over to Miguel and said, "As soon as we can get out of here, let's meet at my apartment."

"You got it," said Miguel, equally impatient and wanting to get this over with.

There was a lot of angry murmuring around them and talk of increasing human control over clone communities. This concern needed to be addressed and squelched soon. Johann feared retaliation toward the clones and possibly an attempted breach of their closed communities.

After three and one half agonizing hours with much emotion and adversity, it was over. Johann gave his condolences to the family and shook hands with many dignitaries and attendees before he managed to flee to his waiting car.

"How'd it go?" asked Marc, Andre's brother.

"Grueling," responded Johann, exhibiting a weary face. He heard a tap on his window and turned to see Miguel.

"I'll ride with you, amigo," as he opened the door and hopped in.

"Marc, let's go before other derelicts try to hitch a ride," said Johann.

"Too funny, Juan," laughed Miguel. Marc, being part of their inner circle, did not pose a risk by overhearing their conversation.

"So, where do we go from here?" asked Johann.

"Not sure. Let's give it a few more days. People's emotions are running high right now. They are calling for swift and dire consequences for Peyton and the participants aiding in her escape."

Johann gave an exasperated sigh. "I need to put the clone communities on alert for possible reprisals. They will need to protect their borders for any idiots that may try to penetrate them. You know, by law, anyone attempting to enter can be shot on sight. The clones are peace-loving people, but they have been trained to defend their colony without hesitation. And humans know the risk. Their own microchips send off signals of a breach, and within minutes they would be encountering armed clones and instant death. So I'm not too concerned about individual breaches. Now a military invasion is another matter."

Miguel frowned and said, "We must present a convincing message to our people that this is not a wise direction. We will need to convince them that the decision to hide Peyton was the correct one. Unfortunately, now we may have to reveal details of clone life. There never has been any information offered, and humans just assumed clones were kept in vats or pens within thousands of buildings. Remember how we were awestruck when we first set eyes in Community 27. We were incredulous. I knew you were clued in to a certain extent due to your position, Johann, but you still didn't know the exact nature of their existence."

"You're right, Miguel. I was stunned."

They pulled up to Johann's apartment. A crowd had amassed around the front entrance. A doorman appeared at their door and opened it. "Good afternoon, Dr. Christiansen. Please allow me and my partner to escort you to the door."

They pushed past the shouting reporters. They were all shouting over one another. "Do you know what happened to the clone? What are you doing to find her? What do you plan to do to her once she is found?"

Secret Service suddenly swarmed around them, assisting the doorman to make a path to the door. Miguel said under his breath, "Man, I thought we ditched the SS guys." He laughed but was actually relieved they were present. When they were safely inside the building, heading to the elevator, Miguel said, "It's getting ugly, buddy."

Johann looked back at him and said, "Well, they don't know the circumstances yet. I'll give a statement tonight. We need to confer with the leaders of the investigation and clue them in first. That'll be your job, Miguel," as he punched the floor number for his apartment. "You know those guys. But be careful not to inadvertently implicate yourself unless you have a death wish." He pounded him on his back as they arrived at his floor.

"Let's write the script," said Miguel. "I've never had to lie to the people. It's not my nature. But protecting the clones takes precedence. And I can't protect them if I'm no longer in my position." They made a beeline to the kitchen for a beer.

CHAPTER 32

The trip to the UN took twenty minutes as traffic posed no obstacles. "Let's hope this goes well," said Miguel, visibly nervous, as he wiped his forehead.

"Expect outrage initially," said Johann. "Remember, humans don't have any sympathy or concern for clones. To them, they are just human parts, their human parts, not people. Other than a select few, humans are not aware that clones walk, talk or have a lifestyle. This incident has evoked an avalanche of questions."

"I heard people questioning how a vat could disappear. Our news is going to be earthshaking and I'm not sure how they are going to accept the deception."

"We shall see. It is amazing that it's been kept a secret this long."

"Unfortunately, now there will be a demand for more information. Many are not going to be happy with the truth." He peered out the window, sighed as he saw the UN and patted Johann on the knee.

Marc pulled the car up to the curb. "Good luck Miguel and Johann. "I'll be right here for a quick getaway," he said, half joking. Mobs of people lined the driveway and entrance to the building. Secret Service appeared everywhere.

"Geez, wish you could get us out of here on a helicopter, Marc," said Johann, his eyes pleading as a feeling of dread engulfed him.

"That can be arranged, Johann," said Marc. "Just let me know how it's going and I'll have here whatever you want."

They hopped out and were out of sight immediately, surrounded by serious looking, don't-mess-with-me, men in black coats.

The room was packed to capacity with leaders from around the world. Miguel and Johann shook hands while making their way down the aisle to the podium. To them it seemed like an eternity to walk the two hundred feet. The anticipation in the air was palpable. The room came to a complete silence as Miguel adjusted the microphone to accommodate his stature. The international president was respected the world over for his decency, competence and integrity. He was taking a huge risk in choosing sides in this circumstance. His ethics and morals guided him in his stand.

"Ladies and gentlemen," Miguel cleared his throat, "thank you for your presence. I ask for your indulgence and request that you hold your questions until Dr. Christiansen and I have concluded our presentation.

"As you know, our existence in recent years has hugely benefited from the advent of human cloning, which has added years of life for all of us. It eliminated the worry of succumbing or suffering the effects of debilitating, progressive diseases. We have all been deeply appreciative of science for this contribution to mankind. With that said, it has been the norm for society not to be involved in the creation process or subsequent control of the product. This, by law, has been out of the realm of the populace knowledge or concern. We have lived our lives just knowing that in the event of a need for organ replacement, the process was available," Miguel shifted his weight, trying to prepare himself for delivering the shock of the century to waiting ears. "Because of the recent revelation of a donor's unavailability," Miguel continued to avoid referring to the donor as one for a world icon, "you have asked how this could have happened. We could have fabricated a tale that this clone, named Peyton, had met an untimely death, but we've chosen to tell the truth. Dr Christiansen and I have decided it is more important to give you the facts. The truth has had a huge impact on us, and I suspect it will on you too. I'm sure posting a picture of the clone worldwide caused immediate confusion, dispelling your belief in clone containment. "The truth is…." Everyone in the room looked concerned and frightened. They sat motionless and silent. Miguel looked around and took a deep breath. "The truth is clones live in neighborhoods, not vats or cages." A collective gasp enveloped the room. People looked at each other and back to Miguel, wanting to hear more. "They have families, grow their own food and even obtain an advanced education. Dr. Christiansen and I were in the process of studying their communities and standardizing them worldwide. We knew one day we would inform the human population. But not this soon. We had a lot of work to do first."

"What about the missing clone?" shouted one irate person in the crowd.

"I'm getting to that. Please, everyone, be patient." He glanced to his left and noticed Caitlyn's doctors in the wings, not looking too happy. He recognized them from Caitlyn's funeral.

Ayudame Dios, Miguel thought to himself. "As you may or may not understand, each clone part can be harvested three times without harm whatsoever to your clone. This has been verified for years, and there has never been a hitch. Herein lies the problem: In our study, we unexpectedly found a glitch. Apparently, during the creation process, a rogue cell changed the normal progression of this clone, rendering it a deviation from the normal. Instead of regrowing an organ following harvesting, this deviated clone would die from the loss of the organ."

"So are you saying that this defective clone would have died following its contribution to Caitlyn?" asked another angry attendee. It bothered Miguel that the questioner did not even acknowledge that the clone in question had a gender. To this jerk Peyton was an object, not a living being. Miguel felt like a stake had been driven through his heart as he thought of Peyton, Abby and London. "Yes, Caitlyn's clone would have died."

"But instead you let Caitlyn die," yelled another. The crowd burst into cries of anger.

"You have to understand the situation," Johann intervened as he stepped up to the microphone. "Caitlyn died of complications caused by her own lifestyle. The clone would have been murdered. I am not even convinced organ replacement would have saved her." Thinking this line of reason would calm the group, it instead, antagonized them.

"Are you kidding me?" a voice shouted. "It's a clone, for God's sake! They're dispensable. Even using its organs for one time is better than nothing," he yelled, shaking his finger in anger.

Johann leaned over to Miguel. "I didn't mean to out Caitlyn, but really thought that would somehow make sense to them."

"I don't think they're going to listen to reason," Miguel said, noting the crowd was now totally out of control.

The head of the UN slid between them with a gavel in hand. He came down hard on the lectern, trying to regain their attention. "People, please. You need to quiet down and show your respect and attention to our dignitaries." It worked, as once again, the crowd fell silent.

"I don't expect you to blindly accept this," Johann continued, "but you will come to a responsible conclusion once you know the facts and have an understanding of a society, similar to, yet worlds apart from ours. I just beg for your patience and open minds at this point." He looked around at the faces staring back at him. *How can he make them care?*

"So, answer this. Seeing you both know so much about this clone, tell us. Who took this clone and hid it away? And did either of you have any knowledge of the plan?"

Miguel said, "All I can tell you right now is Johann discovered the mutation, and that's all I can say."

A female voice rose from the crowd. *Possibly a voice of reason* pleaded Johann to himself. "Dr. Christiansen, how prevalent do you think this rogue cell phenomenon is in the clone population? Is this a one-time occurrence?"

"I'm not sure," he lied. "I have instituted a program to test every created clone. With 500 million, this endeavor will take years. Normally our rigorous quality control would have prevented this, but human error can and does happen."

The questions persisted. "Do you, in fact, know where this clone is?"

"We have given you all the information that we are able to at this time. We needed to let you know the reason for the disappearance and the ethical reason behind sparing the life of this clone." He fought back showing any emotion bubbling just below the surface. He looked at Miguel and whispered, "Time to make like sheep and get the flock out of here."

They both exited with the crowd still shouting questions to them. They left the building quickly and spotted Marc at the controls of a personal helicopter. They bounded over and hopped aboard before anyone could reach them.

"So buds, how'd it go?" Marc asked with a mealy-mouthed grin. He already knew, as he had the entire presentation streaming live on his iPad.

"Ah, not so good," said Johann.

"They're going to be hard to convince," added Miguel.

"We're going to have to introduce Peyton to the world, in the flesh," said Johann. "I was hoping that wouldn't be necessary," as finally, a tear made its way out of his eye and down his cheek.

"I think you're right buddy. It's the only way," Miguel said, somberly.

CHAPTER 33

Miguel and Johann arrived at the hideaway the day following the horrific press conference at the UN. Leaders and people the world over were still reeling from the information, scant as it was. They were demanding an acceptable explanation for the failure to secure parts to save an icon. They were not happy with the reason given.

The guys sprang through the door, surprising the girls. Peyton jumped out of her chair and flung herself into Johann's arms, so thankful to be back in his comforting presence. Abby was shocked to see Miguel right behind him, making a beeline for her. He grabbed her, and raised her into the air and gave her a bear hug without her feet reaching the floor. He engulfed her, but tenderly as her blond hair fell out of its pin into his face. How he had missed her.

In unison the girls quizzed them. "What's happening? Are we going now? Did you contact Claire and Barron?" They jumped up and down, so impatient.

Johann spoke first. "Yes, we called Claire. She is relieved beyond words."

"You have a lot of splainin' to do, missies," said Miguel, with a grin.

"Oh my poor, dear family," cried Peyton.

"Believe me, they're fine now. They knew in their hearts you were okay. And they suspected we maybe knew where you were. They clammed up with the authorities too."

"I told you they were smart and intuitive," said Abby.

"Now, let me tell you girls something," Miguel said as he directed Abby to the couch, sat her down and settled next to her. His chipper mood had turned sullen. "We presented some information to a gathering at the UN." He spoke cautiously, trying to pick his words with care so as not to frighten them.

"And?" pushed London.

Peyton, sitting on the other end of the couch clutching Johann, listened intently, trying not to interrupt.

"Let's just say," interjected Johann, "it did not go real well." Peyton stared at Johann and started to tremble. Johann held her even more tightly, trying his best to lessen the blow."

"Well, Johann, it's not that it didn't go well. They just want more information that we weren't ready to give," said Miguel, trying to keep an upbeat slant.

"We were ready, Miguel. They just weren't receptive, so it made no sense to elaborate." Johann shook his head in defeat.

"We did feel it better to end the news conference and re-plan our strategy," said Miguel.

"So what is your strategy now?" Abby asked.

"We've decided we need to introduce Peyton to the world." Abby's mouth dropped open as she stared at Miguel, then Johann, then Peyton.

Peyton clambered to her feet. "Are you sure about this? What makes you think they'll be any more sympathetic with my explanation?"

"For one thing, you are adorable, and they can see for themselves that you are a person, not a thing," said Johann.

"So they think I'm a thing, huh?" she asked with her eyes wide as saucers and hands on her hips.

"Peyton, they don't understand. This is the first time they have thought of clones as anything other than spare parts in a vat or cage.

Miguel added. "We just want them to see you in the flesh so the rest will make sense."

Abby said. "I will be by your side, sister. And London too, right London?"

"You bet. I'll kick their asses if they so much as say one obnoxious thing."

"I don't think so, London. God, are you sure you're not human?" asked Kirt, who came in with a tray of steaming coffee.

Heinz followed with fresh out-of-the-oven scones and plunked them down on the coffee table. "Comfort food," he announced.

"Heinz," the girls protested. "You're killing us with your

irresistible food."

"Did that kayaking yesterday not burn off sufficient calories?" he grinned.

"Oh, yeah, Heinz," they all screamed. "That almost got us killed too. Who kayaks at twenty below zero and in rough seas?"

"Well you survived. Quit bellyaching," he said with a laugh.

The humor relieved the intensity of the conversation. They all laughed and broke the somber air that moments ago had permeated the room.

"Here's the plan," said Johann, hating to break the light mood and return to the seriousness of the situation. "We are all going to fly to New York, except for Kirt, which I will explain later. I reserved a TV studio for our private use. There will be no audience. I will introduce Peyton and telecast throughout the world and stream live on everyone's iPads, and wrist pads. I will give more details on Peyton and her world. Peyton, if you wish to stay silent, that's fine"

"No," said Peyton. "I want to speak for myself. I need to give my condolences to my OH's family."

"I'm not so sure you need to do that," said Miguel. "That may be more inflammatory."

"We'll keep that door open," said Johann. "We won't have a live audience feed-back like we did yesterday, thank goodness. We can watch the Tweets and social media responses, though, and alter our agenda accordingly."

"That's fine," said Peyton.

"Now say good-bye to the man cave. We need to jettison out of here," said Johann.

"You mean gal cave now, don't you Johann?" asked London.

"Rats," said Johann. "I knew this place would grow on you, and you'd claim it as your own."

"Not a chance," said Peyton. "Your man cave is safe from me."

"Me too," said Abby. "The thrill of subzero temperatures and isolation has somehow lost its luster."

"Vamonos, then," said Miguel as he pointed to the door.

It took fifteen minutes to get into their gear and out of their life-saving abode, for the trip home.

CHAPTER 34

The studio, off site from the main ABC headquarters at Times Square, offered to televise this monumental press conference. They would staff only a minimal number of carefully selected employees and provide a high level of security with armed guards.

As they stepped out of Johann's apartment building, the winter air hit Peyton and Abby in the face. "Quite a difference," Peyton said.

"Almost warm in comparison," said Abby, laughing. They were careful not to mention in comparison to where.

Peyton wore a light-brown, cashmere turtleneck over a dark-brown wool skirt, hitting just above her ankles. Her dark-brown boots offered toasty comfort. The matching full-length, wool coat with a high collar accentuated her shiny coffee bean colored hair. She wrapped a fawn-colored, wool scarf around her neck for added warmth. People were stopping in their tracks to stare at her.

Abby, in contrast, wore a soft-pink, cashmere sweater over a winter-white, tailored shirt with the cuffs showing. She had on gray-tweed slacks and black boots and a short, matching gray-tweed coat. She donned a beret which allowed blond tendrils to peak out. London followed out the door in a striking meadow-green wool dress to mid-calf. She wore dark-green leather platform boots with a winter-white lamb's wool coat just to the hem of her skirt. Her radiant, red hair was pulled up into her matching wool cap.

Their extraordinary looks continued to draw people who had no idea who these gorgeous creatures were. The murmuring indicated that no one could identify them, yet they were taking pictures furiously as the girls walked briskly to a waiting car. Peyton wore sunglasses to help hide her identity as her picture, rather Caitlyn's, had been plastered everywhere. Within minutes, they were settled in the car and on their way to the studio.

"Phew," said Peyton. "Don't know why our presence created such a commotion," as she took off her sunglasses." She felt slightly nervous, tapping her foot unconsciously.

"You will do just fine, Peyton," Johann said, trying to be encouraging. He took her hand and gave it a squeeze. He knew she was determined to present a positive view of her predicament and he was convinced rational people would sympathize with her.

They arrived at the studio, and as promised, there were only a few people present. A director guided them to a small area where the live appearance would take place. Johann shook hands with the stage manager and said, "I am so grateful for your willingness to sponsor our press conference." He looked around and noted only a handful of staff present, just enough to televise them. The set consisted of a cozy area of overstuffed chairs of earth tone colors and a matching couch. A large bouquet of orange and salmon flowers, artfully arranged, sat on a nearby side table. "Looks good," said Johann.

Miguel helped the girls off with their coats as they looked around nervously. "Just be yourself, Peyton. Everyone will love you. You'll see."

The stage manager walked over to the set and motioned to Peyton and Johann to join him. "You'll know which camera is on you by the red button glowing," as he pointed to a spot on one of the cameras. Try to relax. I will have President Tavares and the other two gals sitting on the set behind you. Will they be speaking?"

"Only President Tavares," said Johann. "He will be contributing to the introduction." Miguel walked over and shook hands with the stage manager.

"Then we will have you both flanking Peyton," pointing to the spot where the three of them would be standing. "Would you prefer a podium?" he asked.

"Peyton?" asked Johann. "Would you like a podium to hold on to?" He had a half-smile on his face, knowing Peyton's knees were probably knocking by now.

"Nope, I'm good," she shot back at him, taking him by surprise.

Johann sure hoped he had made the right decision to put Peyton and the clone world out to the human society. Too late for second-guessing.

"Okay listen up," ordered the stage manager. "Here we go." He held his hand in the air. "We will be live in three, two, one," as his hand went down and the red light glowed on the front camera. Peyton stood just off camera.

Johann looked straight into the camera and spoke first. "As promised, I am here to again address my fellow citizens of the world. President Tavares and I appreciate the opportunity to give you enlightening information that hopefully will dispel the ugly talk that has permeated the mass media. I realize there has not been enough information to draw rational conclusions about recent events. So you cannot be entirely blamed for the upheaval that has ensued."

Miguel cut in. "The decision to come here today did not come easily. We are defying the laws of the world, so you must know how difficult this is. Dr. Christiansen and I felt it urgent to stem any notion that mankind must invade the sanctity of the clone environment and to tell you the truth. Truth that we just learned not too long ago. We, like you, were in the dark as to the state of clone existence. Now you will see and hear for yourself. I would like to introduce Ms. Peyton, Caitlyn's clone.

As Peyton stepped into the spotlight, now free of her sunglasses, coat and scarf, an audible gasp came from behind the cameras. The staff stared at her; smiles spread across their faces along with looks of disbelief. One staffer whispered, "This is unbelievable. It's Caitlyn." Another responded, "No, it's not. Caitlyn is dead, you imbecile."

The social media were in an instant frenzy, buzzing about thinking of clones as spare parts, but now seeing this ravishing beauty.

Peyton glanced over to Johann, trying not to reveal her absolute devotion to him. He nodded back at her. She began to speak. "First let me assure you, I would never do anything to intentionally harm anyone, clone or human. I'd like you to know that every single clone ever created wants to service his or her original human. I don't know why my genetic makeup is abnormal. And I don't know why poor Caitlyn had the bad luck to have me as her clone. I should have been destroyed at birth and a new clone created. I am so sorry. I now have learned that my OH was a loved human being and the whole world grieves for her." Peyton looked down, almost ashamed of the outcome. "A decision was made to take me away so further study could be done and to probe for other possible aberrations. Dr. Christiansen found that after initial assessment, I lacked the regeneration ability and that organ donation was certain death for me. Since I am an aberration, he felt it necessary to keep me alive. Dr. Christiansen jeopardized his position and possibly his life in making this decision." She did not go as far as revealing his involvement in the actual escape and hiding.

"I promise to reveal, over time, details of our very secret society as I agree, it is time for human society to know the truth. It is a lot to absorb and I hope to dispel any notion that we are monsters or only a collection of organs sitting in some tank. I stand here to let you see me as a caring, hard-working member of a very large community." She then motioned to Abby and London to stand up. "These two gorgeous specimens are also clones. We work side by side in a very progressive community. I will have more to say, as I promised, later." Abby and London sat back down.

Johann and Miguel smiled at Peyton with proud encouragement. As Johann turned back, he noticed something reflecting out of the corner of his eye. Without warning, a gunshot rang out. Then another. Before Johann could react, he saw Marc instinctively fling himself atop Peyton, protecting her with his body. The second shot hit him squarely in the back. A third shot rang out before staffers jumped the shooter, who had emerged from the side of the set.

"How in hell?" yelled the stage manager as five guys struggled with the gunman. Another shot went off, striking one of the staffers point blank, killing him instantly. Another stagehand managed to grab the gun, turning it around as hard as he could, putting his thumb over the assailant's thumb on the trigger. He pulled the trigger, striking the shooter in the head, killing him.

Johann was screaming. "Oh my God. She's been hit. Peyton's been hit." Marc was lying next to Peyton in a pool of blood. Johann was not sure whose blood was flooding the floor. He pulled off her sweater and shirt to find a bullet hole in her chest, blood gushing out with every heartbeat. "Peyton, Peyton, don't leave me. Wake up!" Johann was frantically trying to get her to respond. She remained unconscious, clearly losing the battle.

Paramedics were there within minutes, performing life-saving measures to stem the loss of more blood as best they could. They whisked her away immediately and headed to the nearest trauma center.

Abby and London were screaming uncontrollably, clutching each other in horror. Johann was zombie-like, trying to comprehend what had just happened. Miguel was barking orders to everyone to secure the area and get Johann to the hospital to oversee Peyton's care. Who knows if they would care for her as they would a human? If someone was willing to assassinate her, maybe another would be willing to sabotage her medical care. Poor Marc, thought Miguel. What a hero. If Peyton lives, it will be because of Marc's sacrifice. Instead of one bullet, Peyton would have taken two, certainly killing her instantly.

Secret Service descended on the studio. They immediately ushered Abby and London out to a waiting car and escorted Johann to another to rush him to the hospital.

Miguel finally sat down, shaking his head, and looked over at the shooter, bleeding out on the floor. His secret service men flocked him. "How could this happen? Who is he? Everyone had been screened," he yelled. "How could anyone get a gun in here?"

"Actually, he was a staffer. He had a gun because he was part of the security force assigned to this studio. He had total clearance."

"Then why did he do this?" Miguel's eyes were now furious with rage.

"Word has it that he had gone out with Caitlyn a time or two and was devastated by her passing. When he found out her clone would be speaking, he decided to avenge Caitlyn's death. A real nutjob."

"Oh, hell," sighed Miguel. "There's got to be hundreds of these freaking boy-toys around the city then. I want you to find every last one of them and keep them under surveillance. Get their microchip IDs, so we know who and where they are." He stood up, walked over to the corpse and spat on him.

Attendants had put Marc in a body bag and were loading him on a gurney to roll out to a waiting hearse. Miguel followed, then got into a black town car and headed to the hospital. He pulled out his cell phone, placed a call to Kirt. "Hey buddy. Got some very bad news. You need to head to New York immediately. Marc is dead and Peyton may not be far behind him." There was silence at the other end and a click soon after. Miguel now blankly stared at the buildings blurring by him, tears rolling down his face.

CHAPTER 35

Johann arrived just as they wheeled Peyton past him to surgery. She looked extremely pale, hooked up to numerous IVs with blood pumping in at a rapid rate. She remained unconscious, and all life-saving measures were being employed by the trauma team. He breathed a sigh of relief, trying to comprehend that they were doing everything possible to save a life—even a clone's life.

"Dr. Christiansen?" called out one of the chest surgeons. "We'll do everything in our power to save her. We think the bullet pierced a major vessel and possibly her heart, but if we get in there in time, we feel sure we can stop the bleeding and repair the damage." He turned on his heels, chasing after the gurney into the OR. Johann collapsed into a chair in the emergency room. He felt slightly reassured, but wasn't quite as optimistic as the surgeon. The doctor in him knew of any number of complications that could occur. And her survival depended on the amount of blood loss at this point. Her unclone-like properties had now come to compromise her, putting her on the same level playing field as the human race.

Miguel rushed in and made his way to Johann. "How is she, compadre?" He looked at Johann's face, expressionless, his usual deep-blue eyes now red and puffy.

"Miguel, I don't know. They rushed her into surgery. She's very critical and it could go either way. I was so dumb to bring her to New York. It's all my fault. Now I may lose her, and I'm not sure I can take that." Tears welled up in his eyes.

"Johann," Miguel said as he pulled him into a hug. "It was our collective decision to introduce her to the world. It's not your fault. Who could have fathomed some psycho friend of Caitlyn's would try to kill her? We had security detail everywhere. It's not like he was a crazed human off the street."

"I know we could not have thwarted this, but this guy outsmarted us. He knew he was a trusted security agent as well as a long-standing employee with no violent history. But that bitch Caitlyn turned him into a psycho. A sicko. That's what she did to men. She manipulated them to be what she wanted them to be to please her own cravings."

"Johann, its water over the dam. We need to concentrate on Peyton now."

"Where are Abby and London?" Johann suddenly realized he had not thought about them or their well being. Fear gripped him. "They didn't get shot, did they?"

"They are in a secure location under protective custody. Andre is with them. No, they didn't get shot; they're just horrified and pretty freaked out. Kirt is on his way."

"Oh, thank God. Who knows if there will be copycats out there?"

"We've instituted a surveillance program of all the nuts, Johann. I also think people have changed their tune about Peyton after seeing her and listening to her story. They are angry about the attempt on her life."

"Well, just in case, I want Kirt, when he gets here, and Andre, to fly the girls back to Community 27." Johann didn't need the added worry of the girls' safety.

As the hours passed, Johann paced, checking the time on his cell phone every few minutes. He could have gone back to the OR, but emotionally wouldn't be able to handle it. He was too scared to know her ongoing status, but now was getting more frantic by the minute, not knowing. Suddenly, Dr. Mason emerged from the OR. "Dr. Christiansen, I'm happy to inform you we successfully stopped the hemorrhage and were able to repair the tear in her heart. She is not totally out of the woods, however, but the odds are now in her favor. She had significant blood loss and time will tell if her organs, including her brain, survived the lack of oxygen."

Johann's knees buckled. Dr. Mason caught him, preventing him from hitting the floor. "Thank you so much," Johann whispered sheepishly," not only for keeping me from a nasty fall, but for your expertise." Dr. Mason and Miguel lowered him into a chair.

"If you feel up to it, you can come back with me now. Mr. President, you too." Dr. Mason gestured toward the OR doors. "She is still in the recovery room."

Johann still felt weak, but wanted to see Peyton. Miguel hauled him up and guided him through the doors. Peyton was on a ventilator, and had IVs in three ports. She still had blood infusing along with antibiotics and steroids. Her color was now a little pinker than a few hours ago. Johann reached for her hand. "Peyton, I'm here. We will get you through this." They had her in a medically induced coma because of the endotracheal tube. "How soon can she be removed from the respirator?" asked Johann.

"Maybe as soon as twenty-four to seventy-two hours," said Dr. Mason. "She's doing well, but we want to be sure she is stable and strong enough to breathe on her own before we disconnect her lifeline. He handed Peyton's chart to the registered nurse who would be following her in ICU. She was there familiarizing herself with the patient. "Take good care of her, Sarah."

"You know I will, Dr. Mason." Sarah checked Peyton's vital signs and gave a thumbs-up to Johann. "Don't worry, Dr. Christiansen. I think she's a fighter just as Caitlyn was."

A shiver came over Johann. Oh my God, Johann thought. This is the same hospital and, as luck would have it, the same ICU nurse who took care of Caitlyn. He began to get clammy and lightheaded.

"Dr. Christiansen, are you alright?" Sarah asked as she rushed over to him. Miguel caught him as he started to wobble.

"Here we go again," said Miguel as he helped Johann to a chair.

Sarah spoke softly as she placed her hand on Johann's shoulder. "Dr. Christiansen, it is my honor to take care of Peyton. I'm sorry if I caused you any anxiety by revealing my association with Caitlyn. That fact will not, in any way, interfere with my ability to render the best care possible to this darling girl. Of course, our team feels awful about what happened to Peyton and in no way feel resentful about her inability to donate to a dying Caitlyn. Please be assured we will do everything possible to return Peyton to good health." She knew that Peyton meant more to Johann than anyone had suspected. She saw it in his eyes and in his responses. He could not hide his love for her.

"I don't know how to thank you, Sarah," he stammered as he fought to regain his composure.

"You may be a big shot-doctor," Miguel said to Johann with a smirk out of earshot of the nurse, "but you're still a tender-hearted, love-sick frat boy." Johann smiled and punched Miguel in the gut.

CHAPTER 36

Journalists from all over the world flocked to New York Memorial Hospital. Vans with satellite dishes with 6-foot towers clogged the streets for blocks in each direction. Reporters, begging for information, approached every staff member struggling to get through the mob just to get to their jobs. Police everywhere, trying to handle the melee, busily roped off areas to prevent anyone without authorization from entering the hospital. A news conference was scheduled for 4:00 pm to provide an update from Peyton's chest surgeon and attending physician. Everyone pushed and shoved, jockeying for a spot close to the podium so they would be in line to ask a question. TV stations preempted all programming to stay live with this world-shattering event. TV journalists reported endlessly about the shocking new knowledge of a clone world so secretively kept from humans. Questions arising about these beings begot speculative answers. Cable News International IBC's broadcast was typical of the chatter.

"Good evening. I'm Chet Shannon along with our renowned medical expert, Dr. Thurman Keyes, to bring you live updates on the issue of clone beings. This new knowledge will potentially change the lives of every man, woman and child on this earth." He earnestly looked into the camera, and with dramatic fervor in his voice, asked, "Dr Keyes, what impact do you think this new discovery will have on us?"

Dr Keyes, a frequent commentator on the show, responded very matter-of-factly, "First of all, thanks for having me join you today. I'm not sure how much I can contribute to the facts because I am as much in the dark as you regarding this clone civilization. I'm not sure why this has been kept top secret other than possibly to prevent intermingling of the two species. But let me be honest, their creation was just for one thing, to service humans by advancing longevity and preventing suffering. Now that we know they are more than just extra parts and have a functioning brain, in fact, capable of higher education, it puts a whole new light on the clone program."

Chet said, "Some people are saying they should have had their brain tweaked during the process to not allow such advancement, essentially implying they should have been imbeciles."

"Well, I think that line of thinking is flawed at best. These people, as we have learned, are self-sufficient, lessening the financial burden on humans. We didn't even know that our financial contribution to clone care in our taxes actually could have been tenfold if not for the ingenuity of the clone communities."

"The policy has been for no entrance within the walls of the communities. Now we know why. Do you think that policy will change?"

"I doubt it. There will be even more protection for them. Remember, they are isolated, free of the viruses and bacteria that plague us. We can't afford to contaminate them. I know there is extreme curiosity and everyone, including me, wants to know about our own clone. But we must be very careful before opening that can of worms." Dr. Keyes shifted in his chair. He tried to choose his words carefully so as not to give any ideas to hopeful viewers.

"Then, in your opinion, it's still not any of our business to know this society personally," Chet pressed him.

"What I'm saying is maybe it's okay to know about them now, but not to disrupt them. We humans have many flaws, as you well know. They are utopian and certainly don't need our foibles to contaminate their world. I emphatically agree they need to continue to be isolated, with our participation being advisory only. Dr. Christiansen stated that he and his team were in the process of evaluating communities worldwide to assure that all were up to acceptable standards and that the lives of clones were as satisfactory as possible. Now he has the added task of individual testing to determine if there are any additional aberrant clones. I think that is all that is necessary."

"Thank you, Dr. Keyes, for your insightful contribution today. We look forward to having you back again to give us ongoing information about this unexpected historical event. This is Chett Shannon. We'll be right back with late-breaking reports as they come in."

"Johann," Miguel said as he put his hand on Johann's shoulder, "the news agencies are all going nuts over this. I've got to somehow defuse our people at the news conference to quell this mess." All the TVs in the hospital were turned to this event, with people everywhere, glued to the sets.

"I will go with you to add my two cents if you want," responded Johann, the sleepless nights taking their toll as evidenced in his face.

"No, amigo. You stay here with Peyton. I can handle this."

"How are you going to convince the people of the world that they have been better off being deceived?"

"I guess I will need divine intervention." He gave a shrug, grabbed Johann in a bear hug and said, "Call me if anything changes. If you have any bright ideas, let me know."

Cade clicked off the TV, turned to his brother and slammed his hand on the kitchen counter. "This is not acceptable. The International Clone Federation is responsible for this abomination. How many other failures are out there? Is my clone an aberration? We have a right to know," he shouted.

"I don't know what you think you can do about it, bro," said Danyn. "You have no connections, buddy."

"We'll see about that. I guess I'll have to make a connection. Start rallying the troops," he said, indignant.

Cade was known for his rallying and riling. The government already kept a close eye on him. He was never happy with the New World Order and especially disliked Miguel Tavares. What makes him think his constitution supersedes the USA's? He hit the address button on his wrist iPad, bringing up hundreds of his supporters. Another button push and he had them all ready for a flash email. He began to talk furiously into the device, glaring up at his brother with a watch-me expression. "Compatriots, we must gather ASAP. We will convene in two days at Central Park North, at the amphitheater. Call all your constituents." He clicked off the iPad with a huff.

"Cade," said Danyn. "I don't see how you or any of your myriad of cronies could possibly go up against our government."

"Oh, it's not going to be just my cronies, dear big brother. My cronies have their own cronies all over the world. Don't doubt the power of the people."

Danyn gave a sigh and shook his head. "Whatever. But just so you know, I'm staying on the sidelines. You're bull-headedness is going to surely get you in big trouble and I'd just as soon stay out of it." He put his hand out in a truce. Cade slapped it with a stern look.

"Have it your way, Danyn, but your passive nature is not ever going to get you anywhere in this world." He stormed out of the kitchen to his room, packed with all the latest techno electronics. TVs blasted the latest chatter, and monitor screens displayed news from all around the globe. His fury increased by the hour as he learned more and more about possible multiple failures within the clone program. He wanted his own clone found and tested. If found to be defective, he wanted another one created immediately. "If I have to breach every damn community to find him, I will," he screamed. But first I must get to that Christiansen dude and get the freaken classified codes, he thought to himself. Maybe the world will feel differently about saving his scrawny neck once I have him in my grasp. Cade paced in front of the monitors, sweat now trickling down his face. He will need as many friends as possible to invade a community once he has the code with the name and location.

CHAPTER 37

A mix of supporters and the curious started to assemble despite the early morning chill and threats of freezing rain. An extremist segment of society continued to thrive, even knowing their every move was monitored. The World Order Security Agency had enormous data-collecting sites worldwide. One's every move was documented and stored on tiny, wafer-thin microchips. Cameras occupied every living space, outside of homes and businesses, as well as in common areas. Technical devices all linked up to the data centers. Even so, people gathered to hear a dissenting voice. Reprisal from the government was a real possibility for attending, but for this crowd, it was well worth the risk.

Cade and Danyn hooked up speakers and microphones on the huge stage. Glancing out at the gathering crowd, growing larger by the minute, Cade said to Danyn, "I wonder how many of these supporters are government moles? We still have freedom of speech as far as I know," he said sarcastically.

"We just have to be careful, Cade, not to be threatening. They can haul you off for that or for being a diabolical lunatic, which we already know you are." He smiled at Cade, trying to calm him down. He knew how out of control his brother could be, from his frequent visits to the government Persuasion Office. "One of these days you are not going to be given a green pass. They're going to lock you up to quiet that mouth of yours."

"I know. I am their Achilles' heel. But someone has to do it. We have to stand up for our freedom and rights."

"Cade, what the hell is your beef? We have freedom. We can do as we please for our careers and life choices. What more do you want?

I think you are reading too much ancient history, about life before the time of technical advances. Man's way of life has changed, buddy. You just have to accept it. So our life is out there for all to know. Who cares? Why are you such an anarchist? Our parents should have been the ones to revolt. They had to transition. But we were born into it. What's the big deal with you?"

"Listen to you. You have bought into the system like a robot. I'll tell you what's wrong. Look at the latest example; not thinking we stupid humans needed to know anything about the clone system. Hiding pertinent information from us, like clone aberration." He was working himself up into a rage again.

"Cade, even the scientists didn't know about clone aberration until Dr. Christiansen discovered it just recently. It was a failure of their quality control. Come on, we have human error, so this was a dumb error in their process. It happened. That doesn't mean it has happened on a regular basis. Maybe a defective clone slips through every one hundred thousandth time. Big deal."

"Well that's what I want to find out. I think we need to demand an accounting for all the quality control outcomes."

"Good luck with that." Danyn gave up and continued to help Cade set up the stage. Technicians busily hooked up international feed through satellite communication by way of a computerized camera.

Unbelievably, the government did not prevent this communication from streaming live the world over. The opportunity of free speech was respected and not suppressed. Outright revolt, on the other hand, was immediately and unequivocally squashed. The element of persuasion would be instituted on those persons until their thinking aligned with the government. Cade was a tough subject as persuasion never worked for long on him. He would go away for a while, then, reemerge with a new anti-government passion. His followers were not quite as radical as he, but nonetheless, very passionate.

Cade stepped to the microphone. "My friends and compatriots, thank you for joining me today in solidarity." His demeanor was calm and cool. "We must band together to state our objection to oppressive governments, namely our United States and the New World Order. Secrets abound, and in recent years we have been denied our individual liberty to participate in governing. Our Constitution guarantees that our government be by the people, for the people, and laws are to be enacted and enforced by duly elected persons. Now we find that duly elected persons are mostly computers just overseen by humans. The New World Order can now dictate what the United States stands for. I'm sure some of you will say you don't have a problem with that. With the recent events coming to light, specifically the deception regarding our clones, how many more lies are there that could affect our well being or future? We no longer have watchdog agencies because they were conveniently shut down and declared illegal."

Someone from the group shouted. "You're just a paranoid fool. We've never had as much peace in the world as we have had in the last twenty-five years. It if ain't broke, don't fix it." The crowd murmured, most in agreement.

"You don't understand." Cade was now becoming agitated. You must listen to reason. You just think things are all well and good. You and I have no concept of what goes on behind the scenes. We are lied to. You are putting your heads in the sand. You only know that all your troubles will be eliminated and clone parts will prolong your life. You have no desire to understand details and think that you can just party on through life. You are trusting and good people. But think for a moment. What if, without our knowledge, the computers were actually in charge? What if the clones, which number in the billions, were in the process of taking over the world? We didn't even know their society existed until a week ago. What if the human race's days are numbered? Huh?" Cade was now pacing back and forth on the stage, pointing to people in the audience, glaring at them with wide eyes, shouting and stomping his feet.

A hush went over the crowd. Now they were interested in what Cade had to say. Were they too accepting? Did they put too much trust in the New World Order? But what could they do now? It was a little late to be protesting against something they once voted for wholeheartedly.

"I want you to go home, talk to your family, friends and neighbors. Call your representatives and demand answers. From now on we need to be attentive to the world around us. We will reconvene on a regular basis. Trust me. I will be your leader and I ask for your allegiance. Information is the key to freedom. And I intend to demand our right to all information. Classified included."

Cade walked to the back of the stage, ending his speech with a wave of his hand. The crowd dispersed fairly quickly, the sound of chatter echoing around the amphitheater as they left.

"Well, you were pretty persuasive, brother," said Danyn. "Kept under control too, I might add. Not your usual hysterical self. I think you may have gotten through to some of them. I would not count on all of them agreeing with you, however. You're taking on quite a battle, and I don't think many want to get involved. Why should they anyway? Unless it actually affects them right now, it's not worth their trouble. Most are not visionaries like you. God, Cade, you have been meddling in things since you were a little kid, always wanting to know why. I was always tempted to slap you silly. You were so annoying."

"Still think that way, Danyn?" Cade asked with a twinkle in his eye.

"Ahhh, yuh. You're a pain in the ass." He reached over, grabbed his brother in a bear huge and rubbed his head with his knuckles, giving him an Indian burn. "Just remember, I can still beat you at wrestling." Danyn let him go after pleas for mercy.

"Let's get out of here before the Feds decide we're a public nuisance," said Cade.

They scrambled down the stage stairs, leaving the crew to disassemble the equipment, and headed home.

CHAPTER 38

Hundreds of reporters and spectators congregated at the front entrance of the hospital awaiting the scheduled news conference. Miguel suddenly emerged from the hospital door, flanked by two doctors and secret service men who were nervously eyeing the crowd. Crowd-control units swarmed the area, including the rooftops. Even though firearms were no longer purchasable, millions of antique weapons were still out in society, as well as the digitally fabricated guns so widely used. Underground ammunition could be obtained for a price; a huge price. There were thousands of fab labs everywhere that could recreate a gun to any specification.

Miguel stepped up to the microphone and cleared his throat. No smiles today. Even his dimples were nowhere to be seen. "First let me tell you all, we've spent years establishing peace throughout the world and are not about to accept any kind of radicalization by people who wish to return our nations to extremism with warfaring activities." His tone was clearly serious and foreboding. "Any attempt whatsoever to disrupt or invade a clone community will be met with the harshest of penalties, death included. It would be considered an act of treason and subject to our long-standing laws, which were duly spelled out in not only the U.S. Constitution but in the New World Order Constitution. There should be no question of the validity of this law, and let me again make it perfectly clear, it will be followed to the letter. My fellow citizens of the world, I am here today to ask for your full cooperation in the coming days. We are still reeling from the shock and dismay of recent events. But please, I implore you to display calm, patience, and faith in our world government to bring you all the answers to your questions. What happened to this clone was unconscionable and it cannot and will not be repeated. We are, of course, investigating the unfortunate oversight of this particular aberration to understand how quality control failed or was bypassed and will be forthcoming with the results of this investigation. We are in the process of setting up a federal agency in each country and on planet Gliese to allow each and every citizen to obtain the test results of their individual clone to verify his or her status and identify any abnormality. But understand, this will take time and your patience is vital."

Miguel shifted his feet, still maintaining his confidence and presidential presence. His in-charge image was enhanced not only by his voice, but also by his tall erect frame and body language. "You must understand that we are not in the business of killing adult clones, even aberrant ones. Clones were created to sustain multiple transplants and to live long enough to accommodate their original humans. None of us can hope to live forever, but thanks to this technology, we have a good, healthy, long life. Now that we have knowledge about their actual human-like existence, our attitude has obviously shifted. That being said, we still are not entitled to personally know them or congregate with them." He knew what he was going to say next and felt shamefully hypocritical as he continued. "Clones are off-limits except to classified individuals, including me, Dr. Christiansen and the team of investigators, and previously designated workers. I must reiterate that anyone caught breaching any border of any clone community will be shot on sight." Miguel's face was now stern with no doubt of his sincerity. "I have ordered more border control officers to patrol as well as stepped up clone surveillance on the inside of the borders. Anyone attempting to cross would be very foolhardy and unfortunately would harbor a death wish. Your implanted microchip would set off an alarm way before you could even get near, so be advised, you would not have a chance to enter."

Helicopters from news outlets as well as security units, circled at a distance. Miguel scanned the audience, spotting not only the journalists, but also representatives of governments near and far. He nodded to the ones he recognized. He continued, "Again, the rumblings and chatter we are hearing are not conducive to our peaceful society. We take seriously any threats, verbal or otherwise, to our government, clone communities or anyone associated with the creation of the clones. If you have concerns or questions, you can address them to your representatives." Miguel knew that with the prevalence of listening devices, cameras and digital-device surveillance, rallying against the government would be discovered within minutes. Besides that, moles were everywhere. Information from devices was relayed to supercomputers in nanoseconds. But even in today's society, free speech still prevailed. Computers receiving constant information could identify an individual by the iris of his eye or by voice recognition. This fact was not necessarily known by all, but was certainly suspected.

"In conclusion, I appreciate your concern today for Ms. Peyton and will have Dr. James Mason, Memorial Hospital's trauma surgeon, say a few words and give you an update on Peyton's status. Dr. Mason?"

"Thank you, President Tavares. Good afternoon. I, along with four of my colleagues am working tirelessly to treat Ms. Peyton during her recovery from injuries sustained from a gunshot wound. She is in critical but stable condition, still in a medically induced coma. She will be kept in this state until it is confirmed that she can breathe on her own without struggle. We feel that expectancy of survival is good due to her excellent physical shape prior to the shooting. The plan is to extubate her or remove the breathing tube as soon as feasible, putting her on nasal catheter oxygen. Our hope is she will regain consciousness and continue to heal and increase her blood volume to normal. With the enormous blood loss, brain function can be affected, resulting in cognitive impairment. This is yet to be evaluated, of course, but will be tested when she regains consciousness. Once she is awake, she will undergo physical therapy to reestablish her muscle strength and balance. Meanwhile, we have her protected and the hospital is in lockdown with the heaviest of security measures in place."

"Where are the other clones and were they hurt?" one journalist asked.

"The other two clones were not physically injured, but as you can imagine, were in shock. They are in a secure location and will return to their community. And no, we are not going to disclose which community. That's all I can report at this time, and we will have an update when warranted in the future."

Dr. Mason stepped back and Miguel returned to the microphones "Thank you, Dr. Mason and your team, for all you are doing. I suggest that you all disperse now. There's nothing further to see here. Any new developments will be conveyed to you via the media."

"How much will we be told about these clones?" shouted a journalist from Great Britain.

"Let's just say you will be given limited information as dictated by law. We will keep you abreast of Peyton's condition as we know there is a personal interest there with a lot of love and concern. This is a new chapter in our history, and we will have to absorb this new knowledge. Your comments through social media will be heard. I will do my level best to address all your concerns."

"Thank you all." Miguel turned, shook hands with the doctors, then walked briskly, engulfed by the secret service detail, through the doors of the hospital. Once inside, he shook hands again with the doctors and said, "Thank you so much for everything you are doing for Peyton. You will soon realize she is more than just spare parts."

Seventy-two hours had elapsed when Dr. Mason came in and announced they were going to remove the respirator. Over the last few hours they had decreased her sedation, and she was beginning to stir. A respiratory therapist was on his heels and walked to the head of the bed. Sarah opened the D5 W IV fluid and flushed out any trace of sedation drugs. "She's ready, doctor." The respiratory therapist gently removed the endotracheal tube from her throat. She coughed, which was a good sign.

CHAPTER 39

The snow fell in large fluffy flakes. This truly was a winter wonderland.

Abby pranced into the kitchen, lugging two bags of groceries. She set them on the counter. Having kicked off her boots in the mudroom, she slid around in her thick, warm socks. "We are going to have a feast of all feasts tonight," she announced, her eyes sparkling with anticipation.

Miguel got down from his perch at the counter, bent over Abby from behind, arms surrounding her, and gave a tight squeeze. "Mi nina chiquita, you never fail to amaze and delight me. I will leave you to your magic. Johann, how bout' a game of poker?" he asked, gazing in Johann's direction.

"Not now, Miguel. Ask Kirt or Andre. Not London, though. She has to help Abby."

"Gladly," yelled London from the far end of the room.

"I can't tear myself away from this precious being." Peyton squirmed even deeper into Johann as they snuggled on the couch. He looked down at Peyton, peering into her eyes. "Peyton, you are a fighter, a warrior even, and you refused to let the grim reaper take you. I am so thankful for that. You are the love of my life. We will figure out our future, I promise."

"I couldn't leave you, Johann. Even in my unconsciousness, I begged to be returned to you. The light led me further and further down the path, but then I coughed, the light disappeared, and I knew the end of the light was not ready for me."

"Those three weeks of recovery were almost unbearable for me," said Johann. He took both of her hands in his. "But, somehow, I just knew you would rally and win the battle. That's you Peyton-stubborn, determined and faithful."

"Johann," she looked at him with distress in her eyes, "our battle is just beginning. Remember, I am still a clone, albeit an aberrant one. Laws and culture prohibit our union."

"Peyton, don't let your biology determine who you are. Make it part of who you will become; who we will become. And who our offspring will become."

"Our offspring? It is possible?"

"Oh yes. You are very much human, and I can't wait to prove it to you." He kissed her gently, tears streaming down both their faces.

About the Author

M.E. Shaw, a Registered Nurse, lives with her husband, four cats and a horse in Palm Harbor, Florida.

She is a contributor to a collection of short stories in the book Florida On My Mind, under the name Marge Marante, published by East Lake Writer's Workshop of which she has been a member for three years. *The Rogue Cell* is the first in a series.

Find out more by visiting: http://meshaw.blogspot.com or http://www.facebook.com/authormeshaw

5/17/24

Made in the USA
Columbia, SC
13 March 2019